"We have a history, and it's not going to be easy."

"Especially since the attraction is still there." Might as well put that on the table, Rafe thought.

Melina hesitated then nodded. "Being attracted isn't the issue. It's what we do about it."

He knew what he'd like to do about it. For the first time since they'd met, they had their own homes, which offered privacy, a place where they could spend a whole night together, where they wouldn't have to check out by 10:00 a.m. They could shower together in the morning, linger over breakfast wearing only robes, easily disposed of.

The silence escalated between them. He wondered if her thoughts were headed down the same path as his.

Dear Reader,

Reunion stories pose a particular challenge for a writer. Readers sometimes ask, "If their relationship didn't work the first time around, why should I expect it to work the second time?"

It's a good and valid question. I happen to like reunion stories for a couple of reasons: because the couple's past gives them an emotional footing for the present, and because "second chances" is a theme I love. Combine those reasons with the fact so many of our books feature heroes and heroines in their 20s and 30s, and it's the perfect storm for me. We change *so much* in our 20s that it's not surprising we'd be open to a second chance at love with someone from our past.

It isn't easy, of course. Nothing worthwhile is, as the saying goes. But I think a complicated past can make for a richer, deeper and truer relationship.

Mendoza's Return is a reunion story. Melina and Rafe are plunked smack in the middle of their own perfect storm to weather some rough seas in search of smooth sailing. I hope you enjoy their voyage.

Susan Crosby

MENDOZA'S RETURN

SUSAN CROSBY

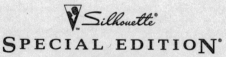

SPECIAL EDITION®

Published by Silhouette Books

America's Publisher of Contemporary Romance

Special thanks and acknowledgment to Susan Crosby
for her contribution to the
Fortunes of Texas: Lost...and Found continuity.

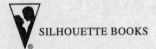 SILHOUETTE BOOKS

Recycling programs
for this product may
not exist in your area.

ISBN-13: 978-0-373-65584-7

MENDOZA'S RETURN

Copyright © 2011 by Harlequin Books S.A.

Visit Silhouette Books at www.eHarlequin.com

Printed in U.S.A.

Books by Susan Crosby

SUSAN CROSBY

believes in the value of setting goals, but also in the magic of making wishes, which often do come true—as long as she works hard enough. Along life's journey she's done a lot of the usual things—married, had children, attended college a little later than the average coed and earned a B.A. in English. Then she dived off the deep end into a full-time writing career, a wish come true.

Susan enjoys writing about people who take a chance on love, sometimes against all odds. She loves warm, strong heroes and good-hearted, self-reliant heroines, and she will always believe in happily ever after.

More can be learned about her at www.susancrosby.com.

For the Broderick family—
Sean, Kelly, Chase, Cameron and Jorie—
everyday heroes. You're an inspiration.

Chapter One

Melina Lawrence looked over her shoulder and winked at her sister Angie, the most effervescent bride Melina had ever seen.

"Don't trip!" Angie mouthed just as the wedding planner signaled to maid of honor Melina to begin her walk down the aisle.

Melina smiled, both at her sister's teasing caution and the beauty of the moment. The church was full. Happy faces greeted her with each step. Then about halfway down the aisle she spotted someone who didn't belong in the crowd—Raphael Mendoza. Rafe Mendoza. Rafe, the love of her life—in high school, anyway, and a little beyond. Homecoming king to her homecoming queen. They were voted most likely to wed….

But they hadn't.

He came sharply into focus, the guests around him blurring into a muted montage of color. Why was he here? He lived in Michigan, fifteen hundred miles from Red Rock, Texas, where he was born and raised. Where they'd gone to high school together.

Don't trip. The muscles of Melina's cheeks ached as she tried to maintain her smile. All of her senses overloaded so fast it was dizzying. He gave her the slightest of nods as she moved past him, her pulse pounding in her ears so loudly she couldn't hear the music.

Don't trip. Her legs kept moving but felt numb.

When she could see clearly again, she noticed the expressions on the faces of old friends—sympathy, but also people's blatant curiosity of a gossip-worthy event.

Angie must have invited him to the wedding but hadn't bothered to tell Melina he was coming. Then again, her sister still believed in fairy tales and happy endings. She'd never given up on Rafe and Melina finding their way back to each other. Angie had adored Rafe as the big brother she'd never had. Adored him so much, she'd gone into an extended and dramatic period of mourning for him ten years ago, after Melina and Rafe broke up when Angie was only twelve....

It was the look on her mother's face—full of understanding and maybe even a little annoyance—that drew Melina back into the moment. She managed genuine smiles for her mother and Gramps, seated next to her, then noted the panic in her about-to-be brother-in-law's eyes. She smiled consolingly at the very sweet Tommy Buchanan, then took her position alongside seven bridesmaids. The guests rose for the bride's shining moment, Angie's gaze locked with Tommy's all the way down the aisle.

The music faded out, then the family's longtime minister asked, "Who gives this woman to be married to this man?"

Jefferson Lawrence eyed his daughter, seeming to ponder the question, until she whispered loudly, "Daddy!"

He chuckled but dutifully said, "Her mother and I." He lifted Angie's veil a bit, kissed her, then presented her to Tommy and took a seat next to his teary-eyed wife of thirty-two years.

Melina went through the motions. She passed the groom's ring to the minister without fumbling, then handed back Angie's white-tulip bouquet after the celebratory kiss, during which Tommy bent her over to much laughter and applause. Then Melina slipped her hand into the crook of the best man's arm and followed the newlyweds up the aisle, leading a parade of bridesmaids decked out in lemon-colored chiffon gowns escorted by ushers trying not to trip over the voluminous dresses.

Because everyone was standing, Rafe was blocked from Melina's view until she was a few feet away. For years, she'd anticipated running into him again.

He wasn't supposed to look this good, this sexy. This tempting.

And he'd come alone.

And everyone there knew their history, used to have bets on how it would turn out. *Now* what would happen? Melina feared she'd be back in the spotlight again, with Rafe an unwilling focus as well.

The guests departed for the reception at the nearby Blue Sage Inn, then a lot of picture-taking ensued before white limos carried the bridal party to the reception. The festivities were well under way with music, appetizers and an open bar.

Because the early March day had crept into the low eighties, many guests had wandered into the courtyard from the main room, but Melina spotted Rafe instantly. He was crouched down, talking to Gramps, who looked so different without his usual Stetson and Wranglers, wearing a tux instead, his horse long ago replaced by a cane, and for today, a motorized wheelchair.

"You're awfully jumpy," Angie said to Melina as the wedding party sat down at the head table. "Aren't you having a good time?"

Melina kept her tone neutral, not an easy task when all around her people were looking from Melina to Rafe and back again. "You invited Rafe."

Her sister's lips compressed. "It's my wedding. I get to invite who I want."

"I hadn't realized you were still friends."

"We've stayed in touch." She clinked her water

glass to Tommy's, kissed him then looked at Melina again. "Now that he's moved home, I thought he'd like a chance to reconnect with old friends."

Shock jolted Melina. "Moved home? To Red Rock?" Her breath felt trapped in her throat.

"A few weeks ago. He bought the old Dillon house, but his office is in San Antonio." She smiled. "He looks good, doesn't he?"

Yes, he looks good. He was a man now, not a boy, and it showed in every inch of him, from his stylish hair to his sharper facial features to his powerful body, fitted into a perfectly tailored dark gray suit.

"He's aged really well, don't you think?" Angie asked.

"Aged?" Melina replied, stunned. "We were born the same year, you know. Twenty-nine isn't exactly over the hill."

Their younger sister, Stephanie, leaned past Melina and said, "It is when you're a single woman." She elbowed Melina. "I know you're famous for your patience, Mellie, but sometimes it's better just to grab hold, you know, not keep waiting for the perfect man. And I do have to agree with Ang. I mean, just look at Rafe. He's like a dark prince stepped out of a grown-up fairy tale."

"That's quite a label, Steph," Melina said, although agreeing about his physical perfection. His perfect height. His thick, black hair, those deep, brown, smoldering eyes that could coax out all her secrets…

"But he's a lawyer, not a prince, and life isn't a

fairy tale. Except for Angie's," she added, lifting her glass, putting on a smile, not wanting to take away even the tiniest bit of her pleasure. "To your happily-ever-after beginning."

After dinner, the official toasts were made and the cake cut, then the dancing began. Rafe still hadn't left. He danced several times, but never twice with the same woman, and he never approached Melina. She partnered with the best man, Tommy's twin brother, Jay, then with several ushers, and eventually her father, who was having a great time in the role of father of the bride. It was the kind of arena in which the boisterous cattle broker shined.

"You fixin' to say hello to your former fiancé?" her father asked as they danced, his disapproving tone apparent.

Melina stopped short of rolling her eyes. He never pulled punches. "I wasn't planning on it, but I won't be rude, either."

"Best you don't go opening up those wounds, girl."

"I don't intend to."

"Then maybe you should stop giving him the eye, so he doesn't think otherwise."

She wasn't aware she'd been giving him the eye. In fact, she'd been trying not to, since everyone in the room seemed to be holding their breath for something to happen between them, some kind of contact. Any kind of contact. Almost everyone knew what their plans had been. They'd wanted to buy the old

Crockett building on south Main, open their law practice downstairs and create an apartment upstairs, at least until the second baby came—with two more to follow. The building was still there, but the plans had gone up in smoke years ago. It had finally stopped hurting to drive past it.

"A lot of water has flowed under the bridge since we broke up, Dad," she said, putting the past in its place.

"Since *he* broke up. I remember how long the tears lasted."

She remembered, too, almost as if it were yesterday. Total heartbreak was hard to forget. "I was nineteen. I can handle things better now." Or could she? She'd only imagined coming face-to-face with him before. The truth was entirely different. He still made her heart pound—which could also be all the pent-up anger she'd held for years.

"You haven't been serious about a boy since Rafe."

"I've had my share of fun, Dad, believe me." She had, too, but she'd kept her relationships light and short-term on purpose. She didn't ever want to grieve over a man like that again. Her pride had taken an enormous beating. Once was enough. People should learn from their mistakes. And she'd definitely learned. "Who needs serious, anyway, Dad?"

"That's my girl. The only thing I take seriously is your mother, and that's worked just fine for me." He whirled her around. Always the best dancer on the floor, he guided her through a series of steps practiced and memorized through the years. Her mood lightened. She stopped wondering what Rafe was thinking and why he was hanging around at a wedding reception, which didn't seem like something he would do, given a choice.

Then suddenly he was gone, having disappeared during The Chicken Dance. Smart man, she thought. If she could've slipped out, she would have, too, especially since she wore a dress that required holding it off the floor so that she wouldn't trip and yet still somehow flap her arms. She was pleased and relieved that Rafe wasn't watching. Knowing he'd gone left her free to be silly instead of sophisticated like him, big-time attorney that he was.

She tried to picture him acting like a chicken in his power suit and tie and his pristine white shirt, an image she couldn't conjure up. She wondered if his hair ever looked less than perfect.

A long, long time ago, things like that had mattered little to him.

And a long, long time ago, *she* had mattered a lot.

Rafe leaned against a tree, hiding out with a few other guests who'd made a quick exodus upon realizing what song was starting up. He and the others grinned conspiratorially at their narrow escape but otherwise waited in silence, not wanting to call attention to themselves and be dragged back in.

From where he stood, Rafe could see the entire room in all its festive glory. The bridesmaids were especially easy to spot. If their gowns had been white, they would've resembled melting marshmallows, like Angie.

She seemed so young. Last year at his mother's funeral she'd looked somber, her clothes dark and sedate, as expected for the occasion. Now she looked like a starlet at a Hollywood premiere, all bright and sparkly. She was twenty-two years old and married.

Rafe's glance slid to Melina as she danced, stumbling a little, the best man catching her before she fell. If all had gone according to Rafe and Melina's plan, they also would've been married right after college graduation. They would have traveled a little before starting law school. Down the road they'd planned to open their own practice—together. Later, when the time was right, they would've started a family. It was all mapped out.

Their plan had been set into motion when they were fourteen. He had lived in Red Rock all his life, but the Lawrence family had come to town when Melina was a freshman. Rafe fell in love with her the first time he'd laid eyes on her. For him, that was it. He'd never strayed. The Mendoza men were known for their passion—about life, work and their women—and Melina had loved him hard and completely in return.

Rafe had never doubted that love. At least not until

she'd made choices without talking to him. His passion hadn't died, it had shifted—away from her, from them, and into his career instead.

It seemed like a lifetime ago. *Was* a lifetime ago. He'd followed the plan, finding more success than he'd dreamed possible, thanks to some lucky breaks, good timing and a few smart, risky choices. Melina had made a one-eighty turn in another career direction. He wondered if she had regrets about that, if she'd reacted emotionally instead of logically then couldn't—or stubbornly, wouldn't—go back.

The gimmicky dance ended. Rafe watched Melina fan herself, her cheeks flushed, her blond hair tumbling free around her shoulders, the swell of her breasts glistening. She was even more beautiful now as a woman than—

She headed straight toward him, across the room, then through the exit to the courtyard. The air had cooled, night settling in. She stopped, closed her eyes, breathed deeply. Rafe inched farther into the shadows, away from the soft glow of thousands of tiny decorative lights that turned the space into a kind of fairyland.

He didn't know what to say to her. Words usually came easily to him, but he had no idea how to start a conversation with the woman he'd once loved, the one who'd hurt him more than he'd ever thought anyone could.

He'd intended to leave the reception before now, to get away from the possibility of making small talk with her. He didn't know why he hadn't taken off, especially since he knew only a handful of people beyond the Lawrence family, who didn't seem to care much about talking to him, anyway.

He'd been debating going to see Melina ever since he moved back, had even checked out her Facebook page, knowing he needed answers after all these years so that he could find that "closure" that people talked about, needing it in order to move on with his life. Especially now that he intended to make Red Rock his home again.

Melina opened her eyes then, keying in on him as if she'd known all along he'd been watching her.

"I thought you'd left," she said, hesitance in her voice and body language.

Was this it? His opportunity to get answers? "I wasn't interested in flapping my wings," he said, keeping the conversation going.

She half smiled. "I wasn't so lucky."

They stood about ten feet apart. "How are you, Melina?"

"I'm doing very well, thanks. And you?" Polite, cool words.

"No complaints." He took a few steps toward her. "Thanks for the card you sent after my mom died. It meant a lot."

Her expression changed in an instant to one of sympathy. "I'm sorry I couldn't be at her funeral. I was on a cruise, my first vacation in years, and I didn't hear about her passing until I got home and the funeral was over."

"I know. I understood."

"I admired her so much." She reached out as if to touch him, then let her hand drop. "I felt so bad that I hadn't stayed in touch. But I couldn't, you know? I just couldn't."

He understood that, too. He wouldn't have stayed in touch with Angie except that she hadn't let him go. She'd written and called now and then, always hopeful there would be a reconciliation, but Rafe had cut off all other communication with the Lawrence family.

"Tommy seems like a good match for Angie," he said, changing the subject, but also leading up to the issue—that he and Melina had been a good match once, too.

"I agree. She needs a Prince Charming like him. He's big on romantic gestures. It was his choice to have the reception here instead of at the church. He wanted her to feel like a princess."

"I was surprised to see how much this part of town has improved," he said. "The only eyesore left is the old Crockett building. I'm surprised it hasn't been razed by now."

Melina went silent for a few seconds then eyed the reception hall. "I should get back." Her entire mood changed, her expression, her posture, everything.

"You might want to wait a few more minutes," he said, spotting a conga line forming.

She looked tempted but said, "I have responsibilities as maid of honor."

Her comment took Rafe back in time—not in a good way. "And we all know how seriously you take your responsibilities."

Her blue eyes turned icy. "And my commitments. I suffer no guilt from what I did, from the choice I made. My grandparents needed me. I acted honorably. Can you say the same?" She gathered her skirt with both hands and swept past him, leaving a trail of unfamiliar perfume and righteous indignation in her wake.

What the hell did that mean? How had he acted dishonorably? *She'd* dropped the ball, not him.

Rafe swiped a hand down his face. He should've trusted his instincts and stayed away. Or at the least left after congratulating the happy couple. This wasn't the time or place for a serious dissection of a painful time in his and Melina's past.

The desire to satisfy his curiosity about her had overruled his usual caution and common sense, dredging up memories that should've been buried long ago—for both of them. He'd thought his were expunged. He'd assumed hers were.

As a lawyer he should've known better than to assume anything. Ever.

Chapter Two

Sunday passed in a blur for Melina. First came a wedding breakfast with just the Lawrence and Buchanan families, then Melina and Jay, Tommy's brother and the best man, drove the newlyweds to the San Antonio airport for their flight to Hawaii.

They all stood at the curb of the departure area, unloading luggage and saying goodbye.

"I saw you and Rafe talking," Angie said into Melina's ear as they hugged. "Are you going to see him again?"

"Red Rock is a small town."

"That's not what I meant."

Melina smiled, not giving her sister an answer—maybe because Melina didn't know the answer herself.

"I told him about Elliot," Angie said, her voice overly casual.

"Angie! Why would you do that? He's our patient. You can't—"

"I didn't give Rafe specifics. He knows you're an occupational therapist, and he gets the whole privacy thing. I didn't tell him Elliot's name or the names of any other pertinent people involved. I asked hypothetical questions because he's a lawyer, and I thought he could help."

Hope battled irritation at her sister for overstepping her position as Melina's administrative assistant. "What did he say?"

"That it's not his field of expertise."

Melina felt her jaw drop. "That's it? He had no opinion as a human being? As a former ballplayer? As a former little boy with big dreams?" Her voice rose with each question so that Tommy and his brother Jay turned and stared.

"I'm only telling you what happened, Melina. Geez, calm down. I didn't ask him for his opinion or advice *except* as a lawyer. Don't get mad at him. Again."

She'd been over being mad at him—or so she thought until she'd seen him yesterday. Then a tidal wave of emotion had swamped her. She wasn't drowning now, but she sure was being beaten up by the waves.

"Anyway, you didn't let me finish. He said if you want to talk to him about it, you should call him."

"When did this happen?"

"As he was telling me goodbye at the wedding. He said he'd been thinking about it."

Could she get him involved? Melina wondered. Given their history, could she ask it of him?

"And don't be mad at me, either, okay?" Angie said, grabbing Melina's hands. "I wouldn't be able to enjoy my honeymoon if I knew you were upset with me." She batted her eyes playfully.

Melina laughed. "Right. Like that's going to happen."

She grinned. "I told Steph not to change one thing in the office while I'm gone. I'm the one who's been working for you for four years, but I know our little sister. She'll think she has a better way to organize things."

"I won't let her. I promise."

"The plane will leave without us, Mrs. Buchanan," Tommy said. "And I'm anxious to get lei'd, you know." He winked and pretended to drop a lei around her neck, Angie's laughter joining his to make music together. With a last hug goodbye for everyone, they ran into the terminal without a look back.

Tears stung Melina's eyes as she watched them, madly in love and happy to show the world.

"How about we go somewhere for lunch?" Jay asked as they headed out the airport.

"No, thanks. I'm still full from breakfast."

"How 'bout we go to your place and have ourselves a little fun?"

Tommy's twin was twenty-two years old. He'd been coming on to Melina since they'd first been paired up for wedding events. "No, thanks."

He eyed her. "You know, I've been hearing for a long time how the best man hooks up with the maid of honor at these things. You're real pretty, Melina. I think I'm okay looking myself. So, why not go for it? Your age doesn't matter to me, if that's what you're worrying about."

She couldn't help but laugh. "Well, I'm honored, Jay, truly I am. But the answer's the same." Between his comments and Stephanie's at the wedding, Melina felt ancient. "It's sweet of you to ask, though."

"No harm in it," he said, appeased.

They didn't have much to say after that. He dropped her off at her townhouse, and she was grateful to plop onto her sofa and close her eyes, relishing the peace and quiet now that her duties were over. But soon the pull began—the memories of days gone by, the should'ves and could'ves.

She dragged out two cartons from the back of her storage closet, untouched for years. She had thrown away a lot of the things Rafe had given her—a stuffed armadillo, dried corsages and a half-used bottle of perfume she couldn't bear to wear again—but she hadn't been able to part with the yearbooks and scrapbooks.

Or the gold locket he'd given her after they'd made love for the first time.

Melina ignored the tiny jewel box lodged in the

corner of the carton until after she'd skimmed through the books, afraid to take a deeper look. Almost every personal note in her yearbooks was a comment on her and Rafe as a couple and their future together. She'd almost forgotten how much like *one* they'd been. Their mutual plan to become lawyers working for the greater good had been shattered before the end of their freshman year at the University of Michigan in Ann Arbor.

Michigan had been a long way from home for a couple of born-and-raised Texans, but they'd had each other—until her Grandma Rose had a stroke and Melina's world had spun on its axis....

All her life Melina had adored her grandma. Being clear up in Michigan while Rose had been hospitalized had been hard, but when Rose had been sent home barely able to walk or talk, it had been excruciating for Melina. She couldn't focus on college when her beloved Rose was struggling, so when the Christmas break came, Melina used the weeks to help her grandparents, then made the decision not to return to Ann Arbor for the time being.

Rafe hadn't understood. Melina stood her ground. And their relationship began to unravel slowly, steadily. While Melina was immersed in caring for her grandmother and comforting her suddenly vulnerable grandfather, Rafe was experiencing the new freedom of college. She'd gone the opposite direction, locking herself into the role of caregiver, giving up her freedom, not regretting it at all.

Except that she'd resented Rafe's freedom, even though it had been her choice to help her grandparents.

And then came the letter from him, ending the relationship, securing her new role in life. She hadn't known how to fix it, so she hadn't tried....

She blinked away the memory. Finally she pushed up the lid of the small gray velvet box. The locket inside didn't contain photographs but was inscribed with the words, "We've only just begun."

He'd given it to her in such a tender way, made her close her eyes and lift up her hair. She'd felt the brush of his fingertips against her neck, then his lips. Finally a kiss on her mouth, so soft, so loving, she'd cried. She'd buried the indelible moment deep, had built an impenetrable wall around it—until she'd seen him, looking handsome and successful and so very sexy.

Melina snapped the lid shut, and with it, the memories. She tossed the box into the carton and stacked the rest of the items inside. Then right before she shoved the cartons into the closet, she pulled out their senior yearbook and tucked it under her arm.

The only way she could move forward was to look back first.

The next morning Melina looked up Rafe's business address on the internet, mapped directions, then made the drive to downtown San Antonio. His office was on the fifth floor of a building overlooking the River Walk. She had to identify herself to the lobby security personnel and get permission from Rafe's office before she was allowed up the elevator, so the element of surprise was gone by the time she reached his office, a richly appointed, incredibly quiet space of dark woods and leather.

One of the things they'd promised each other all those years ago when they'd made the mutual decision to become lawyers was that their office wouldn't be luxurious, that they wouldn't have more than they needed to do the job. The building they'd picked out changed hands frequently, with long periods of vacancy between. As Rafe had noted at the reception, these days it looked ready for demolition.

It had hurt when he'd said that so easily about their one-time dream house.

Rafe's attractive and curious assistant escorted Melina into Rafe's office as soon as she arrived. He got up from his desk and came around it.

"Thank you, Vonda," he said as she closed the door on her way out. "This is a surprise."

Melina rarely got flustered, but being alone with him in his office, this tangible symbol of his success, stabbed at her. The last thing she needed was to be defensive or cool—or let her ego or pride get in the way. A little boy depended on her doing the right thing, saying the right thing.

And yet frustration built inside her, a growing need to yell at him, to say what she hadn't been allowed to all those years ago when he'd broken up with her—by letter. She'd made so many speeches to him in her head through the years.

"Very nice," she said, tamping down her emotions, moving around him to look out his window. She loved the River Walk, always had, no matter how many tourists roamed the area. His view was pretty but obstructed slightly by hotels and other tourist attractions.

"What can I do for you, Melina?" he asked, having come up behind her.

She moved away, not turning around to look at him until she could no longer feel the heat from his body, imagined or otherwise, radiating into her space. "Angie said you were willing to talk to me about a new patient my partner and I just took on."

Rafe indicated a leather sofa. "I don't know that my answer will be any different," he said as they sat at opposite ends. "But I thought I should know more."

"He's a ten-year-old boy named Elliot Anderson, and he has Asperger's syndrome."

"You'll need to educate me about Asperger's."

"It's a form of autism spectrum disorder. They're smart kids, and they can totally focus on something they have an interest in, but they have difficulties socially. They don't tend to make eye contact and don't know how to interpret expressions to understand how someone feels. It makes it hard for them to be part of a team, any kind of team, especially because they can be very direct."

"Okay."

The intensity of his unswerving eye contact made her stomach flutter. She wished he'd sat at his desk instead. "Elliot wants to play baseball," she said. "His father has worked with him on hitting for several years. Apparently he's exceptional."

"And he's come up against resistance from the coaches, Angie said."

"One coach, not all of them. And 'resistance' is putting it mildly in this case. The Andersons moved to town after registration was closed for this season, but the league could make an exception if they wanted to, given that the family hadn't moved in yet. Elliot and his parents showed up at a practice, hoping to talk one of the coaches into taking him on, but it didn't go well."

"In what way?"

"The coach was pushing the players hard, berating them, even ridiculing them. Elliot, who only knows how to comment honestly on what he observes, told the coach he was mean."

"Kids—and parents—often think a coach is mean," Rafe said. "Did he know about Elliot's condition?"

"Not at that point, and if Elliot had left it at that, maybe it wouldn't have mattered, but he added that the coach was fat. Elliot doesn't distinguish between a compliment and an insult. He was stating what he saw was a fact."

"What happened?"

"His father intervened. He explained privately about Elliot's condition, and then told the coach how the only way Elliot can learn about team play is by being on a team. There aren't any special-needs teams in town, only in San Antonio, and Elliot probably doesn't belong on that kind of team, anyway." She paused. "I'm gathering that Angie didn't tell you who the coach is."

"No, but I'm going to guess it's Beau Bandero."

"Yes."

Rafe got off the couch and moved to the window, looking out as she had earlier. "He built that sports complex with his own money. He owns it."

"He's the king, all right."

"Which means he sets his own rules. And he's a bitter man. Always has been, even in the days we played together. But after his injury knocked him out of the majors, he probably got worse." Rafe faced her. "So, what did Beau do next?"

Melina clenched her fists in her lap. "He let Elliot get up to bat, then he hit him with the first pitch."

"Intentionally?" He looked at her in shock.

"Who knows? Another coach happened to catch it on video, but it's impossible to know the truth. People with Asperger's often don't feel pain to the same degree that others do. Elliot just stood there waiting for another pitch, like he does when his dad pitches to him. Beau chewed him out for not running to first, called him too stupid to play. Elliot told him he didn't know that rule because no one had hit him before."

"And that wasn't good enough for Beau, I guess."

"He told Elliot it was too late to join the team this year. He'd missed four practices already, and he needed more practice than the average kid."

"The schoolyard bully grown older but unchanged."

"Elliot's probably been called stupid before, and weird, and all sorts of other names," Melina said. "He's probably been bullied by kids his own age who don't understand why he's different. But for an adult to do it? Consciously? That's criminal."

Rafe leaned against the window jamb, his arms folded. He couldn't remember being angrier at Beau—and there'd been plenty of anger in high school, even fistfights. The competition between them had been fierce, producing a natural enmity. "What's your job in all this, Melina? How did you get involved?"

"Occupational therapists are experts in the social, emotional and physiological effects of illness and disease. We plot a different course of treatment for each patient, depending on their needs." She crossed her legs and relaxed against the sofa. "I help stroke victims so that they can get back to living their lives. Children with autism need self-help skills. In Elliot's case, my partner and I hit a dead end with attorneys being able to help, especially given the narrow time frame." Her voice grew stronger, more insistent. "Elliot can't afford to miss the practices, Rafe, and the season starts in a few weeks. He may be a great batter, but he needs to learn about teamwork."

Silence deadened the air for a few long seconds as he weighed her words. He'd hoped she'd come to him to open up a discussion between *them,* to settle things, that maybe she was feeling the same as he was—still trapped in the past and all that never got said between them. But obviously she'd come to see Rafe the lawyer, not Rafe the man.

"You want to pursue legal action against Beau?" he asked.

"We don't see an alternative."

"And you want me to handle it." Not a question but a statement of fact. She wouldn't have come to see him except that she was fighting for this little boy and didn't have anyone else to turn to. It was the second time since he'd moved back to Texas that he'd been sought for skills outside his specialty.

"Please," she said.

"Mel, I haven't done anything but corporate work since I finished law school. The Americans with Disabilities Act is way outside my expertise. I'm not even sure this is an ADA case."

"You always were a quick study."

He almost laughed. The idea was ludicrous. And yet here she sat all calm and businesslike, except for the fire in her eyes, as if daring him. Like in the old days...

She stood, her eyes gone dull. "Never mind. Apparently you prefer making more money for already

rich tycoons than helping one little boy with an almost impossible dream." She glanced pointedly at a
glass case on the wall filled with baseball trophies
from his days as a player, T-ball through college.
Nothing she said could speak more loudly to him
than that one look.

She walked to the door, grabbed the handle.

"I'll do it," he said. "Or at least, I'll see if I can do
anything. I need to research a few things first. But
maybe even more important, Melina? You need to
consider that my getting involved could work against
what you're looking for. You know my history with
Beau."

"If I had other options, I would use them."

He reached behind her and opened the door to the
waiting room. "Vonda, how does my schedule look
for tomorrow?"

"You're free after two o'clock."

Rafe looked at Melina. "I'd like to meet the Andersons. Do you think they could come in tomorrow
at two?"

"I'm sure they'll move heaven and earth to be here.
I'll call you if they can't, but I don't think that's likely.
Should Elliot come, too?"

"Yes. I need to see him for myself."

"They don't have much money," she said quietly.

"Okay."

"Thank you. Listen, I've got a ton of material
on Asperger's. I could drop off a couple of books
at your house. Leave them on your porch sometime

today, if you want," she said as they headed to the entry door.

"That'd be good."

"Angie said you bought the old Dillon house."

"It needs work, but my dad and brothers are helping when they can." They stepped into an empty, quiet hallway, the door shutting behind them.

"I didn't think you'd ever move back," she said.

"Me, either." He didn't elaborate on his reasons. "So, Beau's gotten fat, huh?" he asked.

Her brows went up at the change of subject, then she nodded. "Beer belly."

"Drowning his sorrows."

"You're probably right. I'll see you tomorrow, Rafe," she said, then left, the unfamiliar perfume he'd smelled on her at the wedding trailing enticingly in her wake.

Rafe returned to his office and closed the door. He couldn't read her. If she hadn't needed someone to plead Elliot's case, would she have contacted him?

Probably not.

He opened his desk drawer and pulled out a small box. He'd always kept it in a place where he could look at it frequently, reminding him how tenuous love could be, but he hadn't looked inside for a while. He did so now, revealing a small, pretty promise ring he'd given Melina their first Christmas at college, only to have it mailed back to him some months later, a one-word note included. The tangible, devastating memory of a promise broken.

He didn't owe her anything, even if she was still the one he'd never gotten out of his system, and still the sexiest woman he'd ever met. But he could do this. He would try to help young Elliot but also wipe the slate clean with Melina.

He would be able to get rid of the ring, get it out of sight and out of mind.

Then he would finally be free to move on.

Chapter Three

Rafe pulled into his garage a little after seven o'clock that evening. He saw the living room lights were on even before he spotted his father's pickup. He was probably sanding woodwork, a tedious process on the way to restoring the hundred-year-old house in a neighborhood where the homes were old but well maintained. Rafe had recently furnished one of his four bedrooms for his father, who'd become a fixture, not always spending the night, but staying often enough to warrant a bed of his own. Luis Mendoza had seemed to age ten years since losing his wife, Rafe's mother, to pneumonia a year ago.

Rafe unlocked the back door and stepped into a dark kitchen, turning on lights as he went.

"Hey, Dad, I'm home!" he called out above the sound of sandpaper scraping wood.

"In the living room!"

There was no evidence that his father had eaten—no dishes, no jumbled-up McDonald's bag in the trash. Rafe passed through the dining room and on into the living room. "How's it going?"

"Almost ready to stain." From where he was kneeling he arched his back, stretching and groaning.

That's how I'll look in thirty years, Rafe thought, although the same could be true of his three brothers, as well. Their mother's DNA showed up in other ways—drive, work ethic, sociability and deep love of family, but that could also be said of their father, too. Rafe missed his mom more than he could say, so he could only imagine the depth of his father's loss.

Rafe had expected to have the kind of marriage his parents had—with Melina. He still grieved the loss of that dream, and the children who hadn't come.

Rafe laid his suit jacket over the back of his leather sofa then crouched next to his father and rubbed his back. "How long have you been at it?"

"Couple hours." He angled away from Rafe's touch and gestured to the entryway table. "Melina stopped by, left you some books and a DVD."

"She said she would." Rafe checked out the materials. The DVD was marked "Elliot Anderson." He took the disc out of the case and headed to his television. "I haven't eaten yet, have you?"

"Nope." Luis stood. When he turned sideways he

almost disappeared. He'd probably lost thirty pounds, twenty of which he couldn't afford to lose. "Is that the way the wind's blowing these days? Melina Lawrence again?"

"It's a business thing. I might be helping her out with something."

"She was gone for your mother's funeral, but she came to see me as soon as she got back." He brushed wood dust from his shirt. "I don't understand why she hasn't gotten married yet. She's about the best catch in Red Rock, that's for sure. Doesn't know how beautiful she is. Loves people. Smile that lights up the world."

Rafe hadn't seen much of that famous smile since he'd returned, but he remembered it, as well as the slow, sexy one she'd perfected, the one he'd likened to her crooking a come-hither finger at him.

"I'm surprised you're even talking to her, though, son. You suffered a lot."

"Everyone moves on, Dad. You seem to be okay around her."

"For me, sure. But not for you. I don't want to see you hurt again."

"I'm okay. But thanks for the support."

He slid the DVD into the player then hit the start button. The quality wasn't bad, but the camera was a pretty good distance away.

"That Beau Bandero?" his father asked, coming up beside Rafe.

"In the flesh."

"A lot of flesh, too. Heard he's been drinking a lot. It shows— *Did he just hit that kid?*"

Rafe didn't answer, wanting to hear the exchange between Beau and Elliot, which happened just as Melina had described. "What do you think, Dad? Intentional?"

"Don't know. Play it again."

They both watched intently, then watched it again. One more time. "I can't tell," Rafe said.

"Beau's got his problems, but I don't think hitting a kid with a ball is something he'd do."

Rafe eyed his father curiously. "You've always championed Beau."

Luis shrugged and moved away, picking up his sanding tools. "I know what he had to put up with at home. Mr. Bandero was hard on him. Working at his ranch, I saw it all the time."

"Well, Beau's lucky that people aren't willing to drive their kids to San Antonio to play ball. Some parents will put up with a lot to have their kid trained by a former big leaguer." Rafe turned off the DVD without ejecting it, figuring he'd watch it a few more times later. "I'm going to heat up some leftover pizza. Sit down, Dad. Put your feet up for a while. You don't need to work all day at the ranch then exhaust yourself here."

"It's the only way I can sleep," his father said softly, dropping onto the sofa, his shoulders slumped.

Rafe closed his eyes in gratitude. *Finally.* Finally, he wasn't hiding his pain.

"I miss your mother so much. The nights are too quiet, and the mornings too empty." He made an effort to smile. "Been thinking about getting a dog."

Rafe sat next to him. "Why don't you just move in with me? You know there's plenty of room."

"I need to be at the ranch. Mr. Bandero's been very patient with me, but everyone seems to think that because it's been a year, it's time. That I should be recovered."

"Not everyone understands that recovery is individual, Dad." Although Rafe had also been hoping that by now his father would be emerging from mourning.

"That's what Melina said, too. She also said I should tell you how I'm feeling." He shrugged. "Figured you knew, actually."

"It's hard to miss the signs. You've lost too much weight."

"Your mom was the ranch cook, and a good one. I can't bear to sit down at the table to eat someone else's cooking, son."

"I get that. Which is why I think you should live with me. We'll take care of each other."

"Wouldn't that cramp your style with the women?"

"I'm as celibate as you."

"That won't last for long." He put his hands on his knees and shoved himself up. "I think I'll skip dinner and head back to the ranch. Thanks for listening."

"Nope. Dinner first, then you can leave."

Luis crossed his arms. "You're a pushy kid."

"Yeah? Who taught me to be that?"

"Your mother."

Rafe laughed, slung an arm over his father's shoulders and headed to the kitchen, the only completely remodeled room in the house. He lingered over pizza and beer with his dad, getting him to open up more, trying to figure out if there was a way to help his father then deciding he was already doing it. He'd made the right decision, moving back to Red Rock, being there for his dad, which mattered even more than Rafe had thought.

After his father drove away, Rafe watched the video again. He sat on the sofa and opened one of the books Melina had dropped off, but he couldn't focus on it, and he'd already researched a lot himself.

Seeing Beau on video brought back memories Rafe had put aside. He didn't want to think about them now, either, didn't want the memories to affect what he did regarding Elliot. Rafe and Beau had been baseball rivals since they were kids, the intensity fierce and unrelenting, but Rafe needed to ignore that for now. Would Beau do the same?

Restless, Rafe took off for a walk. Although Red Rock had grown substantially since he was a child, it was still a small town, easy to negotiate on foot. He came to Red, the restaurant owned by his aunt and uncle. The classy eatery was closed on Monday, so Rafe didn't stop. A little farther down the street he came across Melina's office, a small, rustic storefront with a shingle that read simply Red Rock Occupational Therapy Group, Melina Lawrence and Quanah Ruiz, AOTA-Certified Therapists, Specializing in Stroke Rehabilitation and Autism Spectrum Disorders.

The blinds were shut, but Rafe had glanced inside once before and knew it had a small lobby where Angie worked as administrative assistant, and a doorway leading to whatever other office space was in the back.

By asking around a little, he learned that Melina lived around the corner in a twelve-unit townhouse complex, her two-bedroom end unit purchased less than a year ago. What he didn't know was her phone number.

He'd been headed to her place when he'd left his house. He just hadn't admitted it to himself.

Rafe used his cell phone to call Information, but she wasn't listed. He tucked his phone back in his pocket then kept walking until he was in front of her building. Lights were still on downstairs, but he really couldn't just drop in on her.

Or could he?

It was nine-thirty. Was that too late? He hesitated a little longer, then decided to go home. He had questions for her and had planned to catch her at her office the next day before the meeting with the Andersons. It was better to just stick with the plan.

Rafe took about ten steps, stopped, then turned around and made his way into the courtyard of her complex, ignoring the chastising voice in his head. Steam rose from a narrow, rectangular, lighted pool. Someone was swimming laps, but it couldn't be Melina, because she had a paralyzing fear of the water after a childhood experience.

He moved around the courtyard as unobtrusively as possible, spotted the door to her unit then hesitated again. He had no idea how she would react to his just dropping in, yet for a reason he couldn't articulate, he wanted to know.

"Rafe?"

He spun around. Melina was resting her arms on the pool's edge, staring at him.

"What are you doing here?" she asked.

"You're swimming," he said in amazement, moving closer. "You never even liked bathtubs."

"Hand me my towel, would you?" she asked, pointing to one on a chair nearby. She swam to the steps and climbed out, her bright blue one-piece suit clinging like a second skin, her breasts firm, her nipples hard, her wet skin shiny.

He'd almost forgotten how perfectly built she was, not lithe and athletic but curvy and lush. They hadn't slept together all that many times, at least not overnight, but he'd loved being able to wrap himself around her in bed and touch her whenever he wanted. The few times they'd been able to afford a motel room, it'd seemed as if they'd made love more times than there were hours in the night. Otherwise, their dorm rooms had allowed for only quick get-togethers, pleasurable but not as satisfying.

Now, standing in front of her, Rafe opened her towel and draped it around her. He was more than a little tempted to pull her against him and rub her through the towel to dry her off.

"What are you doing here?" she asked again, not moving away but wariness settling in her eyes.

"I was out for a walk."

Still she didn't try to put space between them, as if frozen in place. He took it as a sign, inching closer, memories of her consuming him. His gaze dropped to her parted lips, her breath coming softly, quickly. He bent toward her....

Melina spun away from him. "Let's go inside," she said, pulling her towel tightly around her, then pressing the button for the electric pool cover.

Her body ached for him even as she called herself every kind of idiot. She'd almost kissed him, almost forgotten why they weren't together. If she hadn't come to her senses— She didn't even want to think about it.

Melina was trembling as she walked to her house, cold from the night air, but she'd also pushed herself hard in the pool. Seeing Rafe this morning had set her on edge all day. Caught between the past and present, she'd barely been able to focus on anything. Even Big John had called her on it—and if a sixty-two-year-old cantankerous stroke recovery patient noticed, it was a sure thing that everyone else she'd worked with today would've seen a different Melina.

"I'll be right back," she said to Rafe once they were inside her living room, then she hurried up the stairs to her bedroom, stripped off her suit and grabbed her jeans and a sweatshirt.

In a hurry, she knocked her robe off the hook in the closet. Her gaze landed on the framed letter that had hung under her robe. The letter he'd sent all those years ago. She'd finally stopped noticing it—until just this moment. Now it seemed to have its own spotlight.

She didn't have to read it to know what it said, as it was burned in her memory. She'd framed and hung it to remind her of what could happen if she let someone hold her heart, as he had done.

She closed her eyes for a few seconds. He hadn't even called her. After all those years, all that love, and he hadn't even felt that he owed her a phone call ending their relationship.

It all came back to her in one stab-in-the-heart moment—all the pain, all the loneliness, all the anger. And now she had to go downstairs and face him as if nothing was wrong.

It's been ten years, she reminded herself. *You're not the same person. He isn't, either. Let it go. Just let it go.*

She towel-dried her hair, stared in the mirror for a few seconds, then padded downstairs. He was thumbing through the yearbook she'd left on the coffee table.

"It seems so long ago." Rafe straightened, no discernible emotion on his face, even though she remembered that the book had been open to the homecoming photos, when they were crowned king and queen.

"A lot of life has happened since then, that's for sure," she said casually. "Would you like something to drink?"

"I'm okay, thanks."

She went into the kitchen, separated from the living room by an open bar counter. She poured herself a glass of water, more to keep distance between them than because of any real thirst.

"When'd you learn to swim?" he asked, leaning against the countertop.

"A couple of years ago. I'd watched so many people conquer fears in order to recover from debilitating diseases or injuries that I decided it was hypocritical of me not to defeat my own." Of course, she'd also advised a lot of her patients to forgive those people responsible for causing them pain and yet she had never forgiven Rafe—which was also hypocritical. The framed letter was proof of that. "It took me over a year of lessons twice a week."

"Good for you. So, the nightmares stopped, too?"

"For the most part. I can still see my cousin drowning, but now I see myself diving in and saving her instead of standing by helplessly."

"You were five years old when it happened, Melina."

"I know." And the impact of the experience had changed her life for years. She'd never spent a hot summer day in the river as a teenager. Never even splashed in a kiddie pool as a child.

Melina set down her water glass. "Why are you here?"

He didn't answer right away, as if gauging her mood. She knew how to keep her expression blank, even though she wanted him to leave. She didn't want to picture him in her house—or to give in to temptation again. Because no matter how much pain still lingered, she couldn't escape the attraction that was still there, powerful and tempting. She'd wanted to kiss him by the pool. Turning away had been close to impossible.

"I had a few questions before we meet with the Andersons tomorrow," he said. "I would've called but I didn't have your number."

"Yet you know where I live."

"Some information is easier to obtain than others. I'm guessing you don't have a landline, that you use only your cell? Anyway, can you find out when the team is practicing again? And is there a way you could get me a team roster, as well?"

"I'll put my spies to work on it." She crossed her arms. "Anything else?"

A few beats passed. "If this is making you uncomfortable, I can call you tomorrow at your office."

She looked at the counter for a moment. She could so easily slip back into the part of their relationship that had worked so well—talking. At least until the very end. Until then they'd talked all the time, about anything and everything. She'd missed that so much, even the occasional argument.

"It's just weird, Rafe. I haven't seen you in all these years, and then…" She gestured toward the pool and their almost-kiss. "We need to keep it just business between us. So, do you have more questions?"

He slid his hands into his pockets, signaling something, but she wasn't sure what.

"In your professional opinion, *should* we be fighting for Elliot to play ball? Will he be able to do okay at it?"

"His having Asperger's won't prevent ultimate success, but it will take him longer to learn and he needs more intensive, individual work, which his father has been giving him."

"For batting, you said. But what about the other skills, like catching and fielding?"

"I honestly don't know. I only know that he can't learn to be part of a team without *being* on a team. It's the socialization process that's hard. But, most important, Elliot wants to be part of it. He's enamored with the idea of playing ball. He says over and over that he wants to be with *them,* meaning the other kids." Needing to do something, she set her glass in the sink. "That drive, that need, can take him far. He just requires more help than the average kid to get there. And perhaps success might be measured a little differently than with other children, but doesn't he deserve that chance?"

"Are you sure you didn't go to law school, after all?" he asked.

She didn't appreciate the reminder, but she didn't call him on it. "I hope that means I've swayed you, because he needs an impartial advocate."

"I'll let you know tomorrow after I've met him and his parents, and dug around a little more."

When she didn't respond, he glanced at her kitchen clock. "I'd better get going. If you can get that info and fax or email it to me before we meet, I'd appreciate it."

She nodded, then followed him to the front door, noting how he'd taken one last glance at the yearbook, in the same way she had with his trophy case in his office. He was holding back, just as she was, she realized. There were things that needed saying, and at some point they would have to be said.

But first things first. Elliot was more important than long-buried emotions. It wasn't like her to hold so much inside, but it was necessary this time.

She held the front door open as Rafe stepped outside. One safety light stayed spotlighted on the pool all night, even though a decorative metal fence prevented anyone from accidentally falling in.

"Did you get the material I left with your dad?" she asked.

"I've already watched the DVD several times. I wish it was more definitive." He turned to face her. She was unable to read his expression. "Good night, Melina."

Her throat closed. The way her porch light spilled onto him took her back to all the times they'd kissed good-night by her front door. She hadn't known disappointment then—or loss. She'd come to hate him since then for that.

And yet she wanted to haul him upstairs and make love with him.

She'd heard it said that there was a fine line between love and hate. Walking that tightrope between those two emotions was too risky, especially without a net.

"Good night," she said, then shut the door, burdened with doubt that she could work with him, but knowing she had no choice.

For Elliot's sake she had to put her personal feelings aside for now.

For *her* sake she needed to lock those feelings away forever.

Chapter Four

Melina had just finished making the introductions the next day at Rafe's office when Elliot Anderson, who'd taken a seat on the sofa between his parents, hopped back up and rushed to the glass case on Rafe's wall. "Wow! Look at all the trophies, Dad. They're awesome!"

Steve Anderson sent a look of amusement to Rafe then followed his son, coming up behind him. He was a smaller version of his father, both sporting matching crew cuts.

Rafe joined them, grateful for the icebreaker of the trophies. "I see you're an Alex Rodriguez fan, Elliot. That's a cool jersey you've got on."

"A-Rod, yeah. Number thirteen. First-round pick of the 1993 draft. He never went to college. The Seattle

Mariners signed him. Then the Texas Rangers. My dad took me to see him play but I was too little to remember. I got pictures, though. The New York Yankees got him now. His batting average is—"

"Not now, Elliot," his father said. "We're here to talk to Mr. Mendoza."

"I know. We looked him up on Google." Energy and excitement burst from him. "Rafe Mendoza was a pitcher for Red Rock High School. His senior year his ERA was 2.28. His batting average was .432. He got forty-six RBIs and six home runs. He struck out 205 and walked forty-two. He went to college at the University of Michigan on a baseball scholarship. His ERA was—"

"Elliot, *this* is Rafe Mendoza."

"I know, Dad. He had 362 at bats, and—"

"Would you like to hold one of the trophies, Elliot?" Rafe asked. Melina had told him that the best way stop a running commentary was to redirect him.

"Yes!" He bounced up and down. "Can I choose which one? I want that one," he said, indicating the very large MVP trophy from Rafe's senior year at Michigan.

"How about one you can hold in your lap instead?" Rafe asked, pulling down a smaller but fancier trophy, one with brass pennants and other game paraphernalia replicas.

"Okay!"

"Go sit next to Mom," Steve Anderson said.

Elliot ran to the couch, leaped into the air, turning at the same time, and plopped, grinning. He accepted the trophy and began to examine every inch of it.

Rafe moved his chair in front of his desk, removing the barrier that sometimes stifled conversation. "I hear you're a good baseball player yourself, Elliot."

"My batting average is .754. That's higher than Rafe Mendoza. My dad is teaching me how to pitch."

"Do you like to pitch?"

"Yes, yes, yes. But I like to hit more. My batting average is .754."

"Can you catch fly balls?"

"Sometimes." He seemed to be studying something in particular on the trophy. "I have to wear sunglasses. I like to wear sunglasses. I like to wear uniforms, too, like the other kids. I want to be on the team."

"What's your favorite thing about baseball?"

"I want to be with the kids." He stopped examining the trophy and looked at the prize case again. "I want pictures like that on my wall to look at all the time."

There were several team photos in the case—Rafe's high school and college teams, all-star games, too. He understood Elliot's desire to be part of something that united people in a common effort, one that brought acceptance and camaraderie. Until Rafe had moved back to Red Rock, he'd been part of some business teams in Ann Arbor, as corporate counsel. Going solo was taking some getting used to.

Rafe asked a few more questions, received enthusiastic and hopeful answers, then he wanted to speak to the parents without Elliot present. Melina offered to wait in the lobby with him, but his mother took him, instead, saying that her husband could speak for both of them.

"I've watched the video of Beau pitching to Elliot and hitting him," Rafe said to Steve Anderson. "Did you have a better angle? Do you think it was intentional?"

"I don't know. He didn't throw really hard, but Elliot had a sore spot on his hip because of it."

"How did Beau react after he'd hit Elliot? I heard what Beau said, but the video was being filmed from too far away for me to see his expression."

"I was too busy trying to keep my wife from charging him to notice." Steve Anderson smiled grimly. "She was seeing red."

Unexpected protective instincts rose up in Rafe, too. Elliot deserved better. "What can you tell me as his parent about him joining the team? I need to know what my argument is."

"Elliot learns from experience, not what people say, but by trial and error—not by being shown, but doing, again and again."

"How does he deal with mistakes? Will it make him put the brakes on, or will he be able to just keep going? Everyone goofs, and it's important to just keep on playing. Can he do that or does he freeze?"

"I can't give you just one answer," Steve said. "He gets frustrated by different kinds of things. Those are lessons for him. We talk about it and try to work it out."

Rafe looked at Melina. "In your opinion, could the experience hurt him in any way?"

"He's behind, but he's bursting with determination. This is his passion. He'll work harder than most, I'm sure. It'll be really good for him socially to be part of a team. Fitting in is important to him."

"Honestly, Mr. Mendoza," Steve said. "I don't think Bandero is going to give an inch. And since he owns the place, he's free to do whatever he wants. I don't want Elliot to be a topic of discussion around town, especially since we've just moved here and haven't even made friends yet. On the other hand, I want him to have a shot at doing what other kids do. There have been enough success stories to give us all hope."

"I've known Beau since my own T-ball days, Mr. Anderson, and maybe you're right about him not budging, but there are other coaches and other teams. Let me see what I can do. Plan on going to the practice tonight, but just sit in the stands and watch."

"We can't do that. Beau has a no-parents rule. Only players and coaches are allowed at the practices."

Rafe didn't comment on the unusual rule. "I'll

call you after I've talked to Beau." He stood. "That's some boy you've got, Mr. Anderson."

"Steve. Thanks." He hesitated. "Can we work out a payment plan with you?"

"This one's on me, one ballplayer to another," Rafe said. "It'll be my pleasure."

"Thank you," he said, his voice gruff.

They all walked to the door together. When Rafe opened it, he saw Elliot standing at his assistant's desk. Vonda was giving him her complete attention.

"Beau Bandero," Elliot said. "Third baseman for Red Rock High School. Batting average .620 in his senior year. Hit ten home runs, got forty-six RBIs, on-base percentage was .716. Got drafted by the Houston Astros. Didn't go to college, just like A-Rod. Called up to the majors in his second year. Played in the majors seven years until—"

"Son." Steve interrupted him with a look of apology to Vonda. "It's time to go."

Rafe shook hands with Steve's wife, Debbie, then he approached Elliot. From behind his back he pulled out a baseball and handed it to the boy. "This one's not to play with, okay? This one is to keep indoors. See this autograph? He was my favorite player when I was your age." Rafe remembered the moment he'd had it signed, too, as if it were yesterday. "He was done playing ball, but he was still my hero."

"Cal Ripken! Wow! It's Cal Ripken, Dad. The Iron Man. He played 2,632 games straight, and 3,001 games altogether. He had 11,551 at bats and 3,184 hits. In 2001 his salary was $6,300,000. In 2001 A-Rod's salary was twenty-two million. In 2001, Manny Ramirez made—"

Steve took him by the shoulders and turned him toward the door. "Time to go, Stat Man. Say goodbye."

"Goodbye," Elliot said, but Rafe could hear him rattling off more statistics as they went down the hall.

Rafe invited Melina back into his office. They stood just inside his closed door. "What a great kid."

"He is. I'm fortunate enough to meet a lot of great kids." She cocked her head. "That was very nice of you to give him your Ripken ball. I know how much it means to you."

"It'll be in good hands."

She cupped his arm. "Thank you for doing this."

Her touch made his breath go shallow. He didn't like it. Didn't want it. It complicated everything.

"I'm looking forward to it," he said. "I think I've needed a change from my routine. Kind of nice to get excited about a case again."

She gave him a look that seemed to remind him that his goal years ago *had* been to help those who couldn't afford good help. To fight city hall and win.

But "I'll be waiting to hear the results" was all she said.

* * *

On foot, Rafe studied the sports complex as he sought out Beau a couple of hours later. It was new, only two years old, Beau having built it as a tribute to himself, using money from a huge signing bonus he'd received from the Astros six months before he sustained a career-ending injury. The complex held four ball fields, with a snack bar and restrooms in the middle of the hub. All four fields were filled with boys and girls teams practicing.

Rafe spotted Beau and headed his way. After spending time on the phone with parents and coaches, Rafe had arrived ten minutes before practice started, but the boys were already limbering up. He'd learned that Beau coached and handled the day-to-day running of the complex. Apparently he micromanaged every detail, from choosing the snack bar food to chalking the lines to payroll, never giving anyone the chance to work independently or prove his or her capability.

To the question Rafe had asked most of the parents he'd called—"Why do you put up with him?"—came the most repeated answer, "There's no place else." One woman on speakerphone with her husband had added, "We all hold our breaths when the lists come out, hoping for a coach other than Beau for our kids."

But her husband said, "He teaches the skills. *Demands* the skill level be high. More than any other coach, frankly. He's just got a big mouth and no tact."

"He's made my baby cry several times," his wife said.

"Which won't kill him, honey."

So, the parents were divided, mostly by gender, and the coaches Rafe talked to were guarded, although one said he'd offered to take Elliot. Beau had turned him down.

Beau sent his team on a run around the field then stood waiting for Rafe to join him.

"It's been a long time," Rafe said, extending his hand to Beau, who shook it reluctantly, as if expecting to find a gag buzzer in Rafe's palm. "How are you?"

"Can't complain," Beau said. "Heard you were back."

"Yeah. It feels good."

"How's Melina? I haven't seen her in ages. We don't run in the same circles, you know."

Rafe managed not to grit his teeth. Their breakup had been big news, but that was ten years ago. Just by moving home, Rafe had stirred the gossip fires anew. "She seems to be fine."

Beau resettled his cap on his thinning brown hair. His eyes were hidden by sunglasses. "Something I can do for you?"

"I'd like to talk to you about Elliot Anderson."

Beau's mouth tightened. "What about him?"

"I want you to give him a chance to play."

"Oh, *you* want me to? Why should I?"

"Because he loves the game. He'll try harder than most of the other kids. Because every kid deserves a chance to shine."

"Personally, Rafe, I don't like shiny kids. I like 'em covered with dirt from sliding into second or falling down as they catch a foul ball. That kid, Elliot, doesn't know one thing about playing ball."

"He hits .754."

"That so? Well, maybe if we had a designated hitter position, I could use him, but all these kids gotta play positions. All these boys have been playing ball for years, and they still got a lot to learn. He doesn't even know to run to first when he's hit."

"About that…"

"Nope. That issue is dead. I didn't hit the boy on purpose. I'd never hit a kid on purpose. You leave that alone, lawyer." He dragged out the last word like an obscenity.

"Coach Wagner is willing to take Elliot."

"I know that. No. Is that clear enough for you? N. O. Rules are rules. Just like the army, we depend on rules. This is these boys' training ground for life. Life isn't fair, you know, Rafe? It just isn't. And this isn't about one kid but a team's worth of others who wouldn't get my full attention—*or* a teammate with the skills to help them win. I've got kids who come from San Antonio. You think it's because I coddle them? 'Course not. They come because I get results. I'm not a namby-pamby, soothe-their-fragile-little-egos kind of coach, and my teams win. Parents and kids like to win."

Rafe respected that—to a point. He tried a different tack. "You're saying you don't have faith in your ability to teach Elliot? To turn him into a winner?"

"Good one, Rafe. Good lawyering kind of language. Point is, I don't have time to work with him." Beau's grin came slow and self-satisfied. "You just can't stand that I got to go to the show and you didn't. You're lookin' for glory through this kid since you didn't get it in the big leagues yourself."

Rafe dug for patience. "What've you got to lose, Beau? Let the kid practice with the team."

Beau rubbed his chin, looking thoughtful. After a good thirty seconds, he said, "Maybe I could, Rafe. Maybe I could. If you're willing to follow my rules." He leaned close. "I'm guessing you aren't gonna like them much."

Chapter Five

Melina stopped herself from drumming her fingers on her conference room table then smiled apologetically at Elliot's parents seated across from her. Elliot sat at a play table, pushing sand into piles with a small plastic bulldozer. Rafe had called a half hour ago and asked if everyone could meet at Melina's office. The Andersons didn't know why Rafe had asked for the meeting, either.

"Have you and Rafe known each other a long time?" Debbie Anderson asked.

"All through high school, although I hadn't seen him the past ten years. He lived out of state."

"I gather he and Beau have a history."

"They played ball together for years and were always one and two statistically at the end of each season. Who came out on top changed from year to year. It created a pretty solid rivalry."

"More than that, I think. But rivalry certainly can spur someone to work even harder." She glanced at her son. "All my life, whatever I've wanted to do, I've been able to. If I worked hard enough and dedicated myself, I succeeded. But no one ever put a roadblock in my way, either. I've always been given the chance—the right—to try."

"Me, too," Melina said, her gaze on Elliot, as well. "Excuse me. I want to get him one of our new sand toys."

Melina walked into the lobby just as Rafe came through the front door. Her pulse picked up in anticipation.

"Are the Andersons waiting?" he whispered.

"They're in the conference room."

He pulled her to the side and said quietly, "Beau will let him play."

"That's great—"

"With conditions."

The way he said it alerted her. She wasn't going to like the conditions. "What does he want?"

"Elliot has to have his own coach."

"I don't think Steve will object to taking on that role."

"No parents allowed, even under special circumstances. So, I offered. I think Beau knew I would."

A hot lump formed in her throat. "That's very generous of you, Rafe."

"There's more. He's worried about Elliot losing focus and being unable to get it back. He wants you there, too, or the deal is off."

She stared at him. She couldn't do that. It would be too hard being there all the time, watching Rafe, trying to remember why she shouldn't be attracted to him anymore.

Focus on the letter. Remember how he ended your relationship.

"Look, I know it'll be hard, Melina. But Beau is allowing Elliot to play and—"

"He's on the team?" Steve asked from the open doorway. "Mr. Bandero said yes?"

Debbie raced up beside him, hope and excitement in her eyes.

Melina had no choice. She had to put Elliot first— no matter how much it cost her personally. "Game on," she said, smiling, heading toward the conference room. Steve looked as excited as a kid himself.

"Elliot!" Debbie called out. "Coach Bandero says you can play on his team."

Elliot went motionless. "I can win a trophy?"

"There are some conditions," Rafe said, including everyone in his glance. "You have to have your own coach to help you at every practice."

"That's no problem," Steve said. "I—"

"No parents, remember?" Rafe interrupted smoothly. "I volunteered."

"Why would you—" Steve stopped whatever he was going to say. "Thank you."

"You're welcome."

Debbie Anderson looked worried. "I think one of us needs to be there," she said. "In case—" She looked at Melina.

In case he has a meltdown. In case he loses focus and can't get it back. In case, in case.

"Part of the plan," Rafe said, "is for Melina to be there, too. For the 'in cases.' Would that work for you?" he asked the parents.

"It's too much to ask," Steve said. "Both of you? How can we let you do that? Your time is too valuable."

"I'd love to help," Melina said. "It would be so much fun."

"There you have it," Rafe said. "Piece of cake."

"Where?" Elliot asked, looking around. "I like cake."

"It's a saying," his father said. "It means it was easy."

"Oh. I wish we had cake."

"We'll stop by the store and get some, buddy. Now I think we should get going so that everyone can enjoy their evening."

Goodbyes were said, including high fives with Elliot, then only Melina and Rafe were left.

"What'd you do, anyway, sell your soul?" she asked.

Rafe half smiled. "Are you free for dinner? I'd like to talk things over with you, get your input."

Melina's internal debate didn't last long. If they were going to work as a team to help Elliot succeed, they needed to establish détente.

"I'm free," she said. "But not at Red, okay? Not the family hangout."

"We'd have to leave town if you're looking for a place where no one would be wondering about us, don't you think? Maybe I could pick up some takeout and we could eat here."

The decision made, Rafe left. Melina raked the sand table, dusted off the toys and returned them to their cubbies. She straightened chairs, checked her schedule for the next day and generally fretted, then finally allowed herself to sit down and really think about the motive behind Beau's offer. She wondered if he knew what he was doing by forcing Rafe and her to work together. If he'd done it on purpose.

Maybe.

Probably.

It wasn't any secret around town that their relationship had ended badly. For years people had been anxiously awaiting a show when Melina and Rafe saw each other again, but that had died off. Too many years had passed.

But it might as well have happened yesterday, now that Rafe was living in Red Rock again. People had long memories when gossip was involved.

They needed to be careful not to add fuel to the rumor

fires that would flare now—and the bigger problem for her of keeping her own fires under control.

She wasn't sure there was an extinguisher large enough to handle that.

Rafe made his way up the street to Red, the restaurant owned by his Uncle José and Aunt Maria Mendoza, and managed by his younger-by-two-years brother, Marcos. Their older brother, Javier, lived in town and showed up now and then to hang out with them, but their younger brother, Miguel, lived in New York City and rarely came home. They had a half-sister from their father's first marriage, Isabella Mendoza Fortune, a surprise but welcome recent addition to the family. Rafe liked that his family had expanded with the addition of Isabella, especially now that his mother had passed away.

The atmosphere at Red, a converted hacienda and historical treasure, appealed to Rafe. The interior and the courtyard were classy and colorful, filled with antiques dating back to the mid-nineteenth century, when Texas had become a state. Paintings depicting the battles between Texans and Mexicans to free the republic from Santa Ana's rule hung on dark wood walls, visually soothing and stimulating at the same time.

As was the exquisitely prepared food, the tempting, spicy scents drifting through the air as Rafe entered, making his mouth water. Even without the family connection, it would be his favorite restaurant in town.

"Hola, mi hermano," Marcos said, spotting him, giving him a big hug. "It's good to see you out of your suit and tie and looking like a Texan again. Did you leave your Stetson in the car?" he teased.

"Actually, I did. I found a couple of my old ones in the attic at Dad's when I went looking for my old trophies."

"Don't tell me you put up a wall of fame in your house."

"Nope. At my office." He grinned. "Surprisingly, people are generally impressed by such things, even if brothers aren't."

"Brothers are more honest."

Rafe laughed.

"You here for dinner?" Marcos asked.

"Takeout. You know what Dad and I like. Give me enough for leftovers, too, please. And a couple pieces of your Mexican chocolate cake." Rafe would take the leftovers home to his father when he and Melina were done.

Marcos had already started toward the kitchen. He stopped and turned around. "Two pieces?"

Rafe held up two fingers.

Marcos cocked his head. "You have a date."

"How did you come to that conclusion?" Rafe started to cross his arms, then realized how defensive it would look.

"Huh. You didn't say no. Interesting. So. Not just

a date, but someone you want to keep private, even from your favorite brother." He narrowed his eyes thoughtfully. "I'll add taquitos and guacamole to your order. I happen to know your date has a healthy appetite."

"And you know this how?"

Marcos shrugged. "Small town. Big grapevine. Apparently you were seen talking with Melina at Angie's wedding."

"So? It would've been rude to ignore her. That doesn't make her my date."

"You're still not denying it." Marcos moseyed closer to Rafe. "Have you seen her since then?"

"On business, yes."

"So, a little while ago when you went to her office? Was that business?"

"Have you got surveillance cameras all over town?" Rafe asked, exasperated.

"Better. A constant flow of customers, most of whom know our family and Melina's. Everyone loves a good speculation, myself included." Marcos gave Rafe a good, long stare. "Dad loves chocolate cake. Melina orders it when she comes here. You don't eat dessert. Easy conclusion. Give me something harder to figure out." He took off for the kitchen.

"Good evenin'. Welcome to Red," said a pretty young woman with long brown hair. She stepped into the lobby. "We'll be able to seat you in just a moment. Unless you'd like to go to the bar?"

"Neither, thanks. I've got a takeout order coming."

He extended his hand toward her. "I'm Rafe. Marcos's brother."

Her brown eyes took on some sparkle. Her handshake was firm and direct. "Oh! You're the one who's come home again. I'm Wendy Fortune."

"Fortune?"

"I know, I know. The Fortunes are famous in Red Rock. I'm from the Atlanta branch. Actually, I was exiled here." She glanced past Rafe. "But that's a long, boring story," she said. "Here's Marcos now. It was nice to meet you."

"Thanks. You, too."

"About ten minutes for your order," Marcos told his brother.

Rafe waited until Wendy was out of sight then said, "She's cute."

"Spoiled. Youngest of six kids and been indulged all her life."

Rafe heard something in Marcos's voice that he couldn't identify. "It sounds like you didn't want to hire her, so why did you?"

"I didn't have a say. Plus she's connected to our half-sister through marriage, you know." He shrugged. "She's learning. It's not an easy job."

"Well, she's attractive. That'll help."

"I guess."

Rafe grinned. "You guess? I saw you watching her walk away—and you weren't looking at her feet, *hermano*." He held up both hands in surrender while his brother pretended to throw a punch. "Dad finally told me he's having a hard time coping."

Marcos shifted gears just as easily. "He actually admitted it? Good."

The brothers talked until the order was ready, then Rafe made his way back to Melina's office. Through the open door to the conference room he saw Melina laughing with a tall man whose straight black hair was as long as hers. He spotted Rafe then whispered something to her.

Melina whirled around. "Rafe! That was fast."

Did she looked embarrassed? Flustered? Excited? He couldn't tell for sure. He only knew he felt pinpricks of jealousy stab him everywhere.

"This is my partner," she said. "Quanah Ruiz. Everyone calls him Q."

Partner? Oh, *business* partner. Q reached for one of the bags of food and set it on the table, then shook Rafe's hand.

"Rafe Mendoza," he said.

"I guessed as much. Melina was just telling me the great news about Elliot. Well done."

"Thanks. There's plenty here for three if you want to join us. Chicken enchiladas, chile rellenos and Spanish rice. Taquitos and guac. Mexican chocolate cake," he added, looking at Melina, who made a sound close to a whimper.

"From Red?"

"Of course. Q?"

Rafe wasn't sure whether he wanted the buffer or

not, but was surprisingly pleased when Q said he had other plans.

Melina started opening up the foil containers the moment Q left. She'd rounded up paper plates, plastic silverware and a couple of Cokes.

"I don't think I've ever heard the name Quanah," he said.

"It's Comanche—his mother's side. You can see it in his cheekbones, I think. For all his imposing height and that long hair, kids respond to him instantly. He tends to work mostly with the children, and I take on most of the adults, but sometimes a child takes a shine to me instead, or an adult to Q, so then we adapt. It keeps us both fresh that way, too."

They sat down and started serving themselves and each other. "I noticed your grandfather is in a wheelchair," Rafe said.

"He doesn't use it all the time, just when he'd be on his feet for long periods. He needs hip replacement but won't do the surgery. He says he's too old."

"Is he?"

"He's eighty-six and in pretty good shape, actually. He's just stubborn. And I don't think he has the desire. He says he'd rather join Grandma Rose in heaven."

The mention of Rose's name stopped the conversation cold.

"Thanks for giving my dad advice last night," he said, changing the subject. "He finally talked to me about Mom."

"I'm so glad. Your parents weren't just married, they worked together. That's a double loss and a constant sorrow. The last time I saw him was a couple of months ago, and he didn't look well to me, but he seemed better last night. I'm guessing it's because of you."

"Thank you for saying that." He picked up a taquito and scooped some guacamole onto it. "I saw him wasting away, too. It about killed me."

"Well, he seems to have a purpose now, which always helps."

"I invited him to move in with me, but he hasn't agreed."

"Give him time." She took her first bite of food. "Oh, man. Best. Chile. Relleno. Ever."

He caught glimpses of her as they ate without carrying on much conversation. He'd forgotten how much he liked just watching her, how gracefully she moved, how her blond hair fell over her shoulders, leaving a curl over her breast. She wore her Wranglers like a second skin, and her deep turquoise shirt turned her eyes the same color.

For several years he'd been mingling in circles where the women wore a lot of black, whether dressed casual or elegant—edgy, sometimes fascinating women who were smart about business and capable of creating software to change the world.

Melina seemed mostly interested in changing the life of one boy.

As his father had noted, she didn't even know how beautiful she was, how wholesomely sexy.

"Are you okay?" she asked, looking uncomfortable at his long silence.

"Sorry. Just enjoying the food." *And the view.* "Marcos says hi, by the way." Rafe opened a foil packet containing one slice of cake and slid it toward her. "Don't look at me like that. I didn't tell him. Apparently we are the subject of speculation from having talked at the wedding and, as of tonight, from someone seeing me come here. Marcos guessed that we were having dinner together."

"I shouldn't be surprised. As much as Red Rock has grown, it's still a small town."

"Particularly when your families have been here for so long."

"Which can be both good and bad." She took a bite of cake, closed her eyes and savored it. "So," she said after a long exhale of satisfaction. "Give me the details about what happened with Beau, please."

"Bandero rule number one—I'm to be Elliot's coach at every practice and game."

"Every one? That's a big commitment."

"Rules are rules, as Beau says. Rule number two is that the same applies to you."

She sat back, looking perplexed. "I understand about being there for the practices, but why do I have to attend all the games? By then parents can be in the stands."

"But not in the dugout."

"What?" She was stunned. "I'm supposed to sit in no-woman's land?"

"Amazing, huh?" Rafe had been just as surprised as Melina. "Rule number three—toughest one—if Beau doesn't think Elliot is ready when the season opens, he will have to leave the team."

"No." Shaking her head, she put her fork down. "Rafe, that would be worse than denying him from the beginning. To work with him and get his hopes up then destroy them? No way. Absolutely not."

"There's no choice, Mel. And I plan on having Elliot ready to play, even if we have to practice every day. I've got enough family to get some scrimmage games going, give him some team experience. And Elliot also needs to learn how to work with a coach, not just his father. It'll be good for him in the long run."

She sat back and stared at him for a while, then a small smile spread across her face. "You're looking forward to it."

"I— Yeah. I am. I used to get into some pickup games with friends in Ann Arbor, but as I worked longer and longer hours, I stopped making the time. I've missed it."

"I can see why. It was a big part of your life for a long time." Melina started wrapping up the leftovers while Rafe gathered the trash. "What do you think Beau's motives are in setting the rules?" she asked.

"It's a power play."

She considered that. "Okay, I get that by him making *you* get involved. But *me?*"

He didn't look at her. "Either he's playing matchmaker or he's planning on it creating friction between us—for his entertainment. Which do you think?"

"The latter."

"Me, too. Let's not give him that satisfaction." He caught her gaze, held it. "Do you think we can manage that?"

"I don't *want* to be at odds with you, Rafe. But we have a history, and it's not going to be easy."

"Especially since the attraction is still there." Might as well put that on the table, he thought.

She hesitated then nodded. "Being attracted isn't the issue. It's what we do about it."

He knew what he'd like to do about it. For the first time since they'd met, they had their own homes, which offered privacy, a place where they could spend a whole night together, where it was comfortable and clean, where they wouldn't have to check out by 10:00 a.m. They could shower together in the morning, linger over breakfast wearing only robes, easily disposed of.

The silence escalated between them. He wondered if her thoughts were headed down the same path as his.

"I need to get going," she said abruptly, reaching for her jacket and backpack. "Thank you for dinner. And for everything else you've done."

He followed her to the front door, waited while

she locked it behind them. "I'll get a copy of Elliot's practice schedule to you, so you can plan. I know you weren't even consulted on this, and it's probably going to be a hassle."

She shook her head adamantly. "I'm happy to do it. Seeing the way his face lit up when you told him he could play. He's— Shoot. There's my dad. He's pulling up. Maybe you should take off while you can."

"I'm not a coward, Melina," Rafe said quietly.

Big, brash Jefferson Lawrence got out of his truck and swaggered over. "Daughter."

"Hey, Dad."

"Evening, sir. How are you?" Rafe asked offering his hand.

"Good, thanks. Real good." He faced Melina then. "Your mother sent me to track you down. She's been calling for a while."

"I had the phone off," Melina said, which wasn't entirely true. She'd had it on vibrate and had ignored it. "We were in an important meeting."

"She wanted you to come for dinner."

"I've eaten, thanks." She glanced at the bag of leftovers Rafe carried.

Jefferson eyed it as well. "Then come keep us company, Mellie. We'll catch up. Your sister's coming, and your grandfather is going to be there."

"Steph's working for me, remember? I see her every day. And I'll see Gramps tomorrow morning,

Dad. Every Wednesday morning, as always. We go for a drive."

"Does he drive or do you?"

"He does. That's part of my job. To evaluate driving skills and see if someone should resume or continue. You know that."

"I'm surprised you haven't been in an accident."

He didn't know how many close calls there'd been in the past four years with various patients. Nor would she tell him. "You know why I'm riding with Gramps. He's doing okay. I'll probably turn him loose soon."

Her father cursed a blue streak, making Rafe laugh.

"Yes, it's funny until you have to live with it," Jefferson said.

"I hope my father lives long enough for that to be a problem, sir."

Jefferson looked into the distance for a few seconds then nodded. "Well, we've both lost our mothers, haven't we? Not in any hurry for our dads to go." His voice was raspy with emotion.

"No, sir."

He cleared his throat. "So, you coming home, girl? Your mother misses you."

Which was code for "your father misses you" or "your father wants you to get the hell away from Rafe Mendoza."

"Sorry, Dad. I can't," she said. "I'll check with her on coming over another night."

"You got your car?"

She smiled. "It's a five-minute walk home."

"Hop in. I'll drive you."

She figured he'd thought Rafe was going to take her. "I want to walk, but thanks. See you later."

He aimed a "so long" toward her and got into his truck as she and Rafe watched. He pulled out slowly. She could see him looking at his rearview mirror.

"You know he was stalling, waiting for me to give up and leave," Rafe said.

There was a lot she could say to that. Her parents had watched their daughter's heart break. Parents weren't very forgiving of such things. "My dad has never been subtle."

Rafe laughed. "Yeah. But he does what a father should. He loves and protects you. My dad's always been a good role model for me, but so was yours."

The words hung between them.

"Can I walk you home?" Rafe asked.

She was tempted. Over the past few days she'd been drawn back into his world, a world so unlike what they'd expected to have together. How very differently their lives had turned out—as a couple and individually.

He'd changed, was more self-assured and confident. He'd handled the situation with Beau without rancor, even though they didn't like each other at all. It took a persuasive man to do that with someone as stubborn as Beau.

"If you hadn't come along, Rafe," she said finally,

"I'm sure I would've picked a fight with Beau, which wouldn't have accomplished anything. I probably would've threatened him with a lawsuit, too."

"Which also wouldn't have accomplished anything, since he hasn't done anything illegal. Yet."

"Yet?"

"Let's take it a day at a time, Mel. Let's try to work together as a unit, not let Beau goad us into losing our tempers."

"I can't even picture you losing your temper anymore." It was true. The Rafe from years ago, yes. He'd been passionate and emotional. This Rafe was smooth and controlled.

"I'm not as calm or patient as you might think. I've just learned how to channel my energy differently." He leaned a little closer, his voice softer, quieter, but somehow more intense. "I'm a man with normal needs, Melina. Normal wants. Even I lose patience when I'm denied for too long. Don't you remember that about me?"

She remembered. She'd loved when he'd let loose of his control, making her feel desired and cherished. He'd had a single-mindedness about him when making love that she hadn't appreciated then, not knowing any different. Now she knew.

However, he was being patient now, just standing and watching her, waiting for her to speak. Instead she went up on tiptoe and kissed him. After the barest surprised pause he kissed her back, feeling familiar and yet new in rediscovery, the taste of him tinder to the dry kindling of need stored inside her.

Can you go home again? she wondered, pulling back, touching her fingers to her lips, then briefly to his, seeing hunger in his dark eyes.

She felt the hunger, too, the need she was afraid to show. But deep inside, her heart spoke to his again. If only his would answer.

"Yes, I remember that about you," she said softly, then she turned and walked away, knowing he was watching her, wanting him, and knowing she couldn't take that chance again. She'd grieved for him before. A second time would be even harder, maybe even impossible to survive.

Chapter Six

Years of practice kept Melina from slamming her foot against the floorboard while her grandfather was driving down Sycamore Avenue the next morning. He was scheduled to renew his driver's license in two weeks—if she gave the go-ahead.

"Next week, I want to drive my truck, not your dinky car," he said.

"I think that's a good idea, except how do you propose to do that since you can't get into the driver's seat without a stepladder? And then what do you do with it?"

"I'll figure out something. I'm eighty-six, missy, not a hundred and six. I still have a working brain. And I live by myself just fine."

"You know they can make you take a road test if they think it's necessary."

"So you've said. More than once."

"Because you seem to forget."

"I don't forget anything."

He wasn't an easy person most days, but he was more belligerent than usual today. Although she'd spent a lot of time at her grandparents' house as a teenager, she hadn't really gotten to know him well until the year she spent living with him and Grandma Rose after her stroke, caring for her. The year that had forever changed Melina's life.

The year she'd decided not to go back to Michigan but become an occupational therapist.

The year she'd lost Rafe because of her decisions. Although maybe it would have happened anyway.

"Seen Rafe lately?" her grandfather asked.

"Yes. He's been helping me with some issues regarding one of my kids." She scanned the street looking for potential hazards. "Thank you for talking to him at Angie's wedding, by the way. I think Mom and Dad ignored him."

He snorted. "I was a captive audience, wasn't I, stuck in the wheelchair for the day, as I was. Couldn't avoid him."

"You were more comfortable in the chair, and you know it. How come you're so ornery today?"

She grabbed the dashboard as he made a left turn in front of an oncoming car, the driver honking several times.

"Guess I should've waited a bit longer," he muttered.

"No 'guess' about it. What's going on?"

He didn't answer right away, then finally said, "Got up on the wrong side of the bed. My empty bed."

Ah. "Do you ever think about dating?" She tossed the idea out casually, although she'd given it a lot of thought. "You'd be prime real estate in the senior market."

He sort of laughed. "Real estate, huh?"

"All it would take is a little renovation, and you'd be good as new."

"You don't miss a chance, do you? I'm too old for surgery, and too old for dating folderol. I've had my share of casseroles delivered since your grandma died. None of them held a candle to her tamale pie."

His voice shook enough that Melina took her eyes off the road to study him. He was wearing his usual Western gear but looked fragile. "You're lonely."

"Hell, yes, I'm lonely. Any fool who says otherwise in the same circumstances is lying. She was the fresh air I breathed for fifty-two years. It's been like inhaling smog since she died. It hurts." He gave her a quick glance. "No more talk about dating, okay? I'm not *that* lonely."

"Okay." She patted his shoulder. "I could use your help with something."

He sat up a little straighter. "Shoot."

"Pull over in front of Howard's, would you?"

"You planning on taking up some kind of sport?" he asked, parallel parking the car easily.

"Maybe."

He laughed. "That'll be the day. You almost flunked P. E. a few times."

"It wasn't from lack of skill but lack of interest," she said with a sniff.

He grinned. She was glad to have changed his mood. And she really could use his help.

After all, an experienced captain could make all the difference when someone was about to sail into uncharted waters.

Rafe had just arrived at the ballpark that afternoon and was making his way to the dugout to leave his backpack when his cell phone rang. He didn't see Melina and Elliot yet, but he was early. With time to kill, he answered the phone. "Rafe Mendoza."

"Rafe, it's Ross Fortune."

"Hey! It's been a long time, Ross. Since Isabella and J.R.'s wedding. How's the private investigation business?"

"Booming. Which says a lot, doesn't it?"

Rafe laughed. "Yeah. What's up?"

"My cousin Jeremy said he talked to you about this baby-on-the-doorstep business. He said you advised him to go to the police and report the found baby."

"That was my advice, yes. Did he?"

"The short version—he and Kirsten did, plus they

got engaged, plus they were given temporary custody of baby Anthony. Lots of questions here, Rafe, and things are getting complicated. No one seems to be who they say they are. In the meantime, I'm out of ideas about how to search for the birth parents. I can't believe the baby was left without even a note."

Rafe saw a woman kicking up dust as she jogged across the diamond, a kid beside her. Rafe squinted, focused…

Even expecting her, he had to stare for several seconds before he realized it was Melina. He'd never seen her like this—wearing a baseball cap with her hair threaded out the back in a ponytail that swung as she moved. She also wore sunglasses, a Rangers jersey, black pants and shoes. Not cleats, he didn't think, but something athletic looking. And the jersey didn't hide the sway of her breasts as she jogged, either. He remembered how they felt in his hands, heavy and firm, and the texture of her nipples when he ran his tongue around—

"So, what do you think?" Ross asked in a way that sounded as if it hadn't been the first time.

Rafe tipped the phone back up to his mouth. "About what?"

There was a long pause, then, "What we've been talking about since you answered the phone—do you have any ideas where to look for answers about who baby Anthony is and where he comes from?"

"Not off the top of my head. As I told Jeremy, this isn't exactly my area of expertise. But if you and

Jeremy would like to meet with me for dinner and do some brainstorming, I could do that. Regardless, I'd like to catch up with you."

"Sure. I'll tell you, Jeremy could use some answers. Between opening a new private practice here in town, the baby and his father's disappearance, he's got a lot on his mind."

"How long has William been gone?"

"Three months. Most of us have given up hope, but not Jeremy. He's sure William's alive." Ross sighed. "Well, give me a call after you've talked to him. Anything you can say or do to help will be greatly appreciated, Rafe."

"I will. Bye." Rafe ended the call and cradled the phone while he continued to stare at Melina as she neared, having slowed as she'd gotten closer, her cheeks flushed, her lips parted as she breathed a little harder than usual.

She wore a glove—an unscarred, brand-new baseball glove she was working a ball inside of, forming a pocket.

Peripherally he was aware of Elliot walking beside her, but he couldn't take his eyes off her. Last night after she'd kissed him, it had taken him more than a few seconds to gather his thoughts and make his way to his car. The kiss had been delicate yet hungry, soft and yet intense, triggering needs and wants he'd hoped to keep tamped down.

No such luck.

He'd driven home to an empty house and sat in a

darkened living room, trying to figure out how he would be able to spend concentrated time with her when one small kiss could destroy his equilibrium so completely.

"Hi, Rafe Mendoza!" Elliot said as they reached him.

"Hey, sport. Are you ready to play?"

"Yes, sir. I am."

Rafe looked at Melina. Her cap brim and sunglasses did a good job of hiding her expression. "You look official," he said, wanting to tug on her ponytail. "Are you, um, planning to…play?"

"I thought I would help rather than just sit on the bench waiting for a 'what if' to happen."

"So, not only have you learned to swim, you've also learned to play baseball?"

"How difficult can it be at this level?" She kept throwing the ball hard into her glove.

She was adorable. Rafe was sure he'd never used that word in his life before, but nothing else described her at the moment. Innocence and enthusiasm danced across her face.

"Can we go play now?" Elliot asked.

Several kids were already out on the field tossing balls back and forth. Beau and three other men, probably his assistant coaches, strode up. "I'll catch up with you. Start the boys off. Pair them up for tosses," Beau said to one of the coaches, all of them looking like high school students. He glanced at Elliot. "Well, what're you waiting for? Go get with your team."

Elliot's eyes opened wide. He looked at Rafe.

"I'll be there in a minute, sport. You can do this. They're just tossing the ball back and forth. You've done that, right?"

"Right." He took off slowly, looking back frequently. Melina wanted to hug him and tell him everything would be okay.

Beau eyed her. "Interesting getup, Melina."

"Thanks. I thought I should dress the part."

"And what part might that be?"

"Assistant-assistant coach."

His laugh started low then grew to a guffaw. "Good one."

Her back stiffened. "I'm not kidding. I want to help."

"I have strict standards, you know? People bring their kids from miles away to train here. Somehow I don't think you'll inspire confidence."

She crossed her arms. "Well, first of all, since no parents are allowed at the practices, how would they know? Second, how do *you* know I wouldn't inspire confidence? Inspiring is something I'm really good at."

"Your lack of athletic skill was legendary in high school. Have you improved?"

"Why don't you just let her help?" Rafe interrupted. "What's the harm?"

Melina bristled. "I can handle this, thank you."

Rafe gave her a good, long look. "You got it," he said, then loped away, heading toward Elliot.

Beau glanced from Melina to Rafe and back again, a speculative twinkle in his eyes. She swallowed her irritation and thanked him for allowing Elliot to play. "I know you didn't have to. I think you'll be pleasantly surprised how quickly he grasps the rules."

"I've done a little studying on my own about his situation, Melina, and while you may be right about him grasping the rules, learning the skills isn't going to be an overnight thing."

"None of these boys learned overnight. Nor were they expected to."

"You're right. Their parents started them in T-ball when they turned four, then kept moving them up the ranks every year. They worked hard to get here."

"And you have a reputation to maintain."

"Damn straight."

They reached an impasse. She swallowed her pride. "Rafe said you want me in the dugout?"

"During the games. For practice you can sit wherever you want." He started walking backward. "I always admired you, Melina. You've got spunk. But here? In this place? I'm the boss."

"Got it."

He joined his team.

Disappointed, Melina made her way to the dugout to twiddle her thumbs. She kept working the glove the way her grandfather showed her as she watched Rafe and Elliot. Rafe didn't leave his side. She couldn't hear everything he said, nor could she see Elliot's expression, but his body language conveyed when he was nervous or pleased, tentative or excited. The other boys weren't talking to him, but they were also busy every second doing a drill of some kind or another, and Elliot wouldn't strike up a conversation with them. They needed to do the talking first.

Then batting practice started and everyone seemed to be holding their breath as Beau threw the first pitch. Elliot smacked ball after ball. Finally after a long string of hits, Beau said, "See that, boys? *That's* hitting. You could learn a thing or two from Elliot. He keeps his eyes on the ball."

"That's an expression," Elliot said. "It means I watch it real close. My batting average is .754," he added, which probably didn't endear him to his teammates, who didn't understand that he wasn't bragging but just being honest.

"Well, you're batting a thousand today," Beau said.

By the time practice was over, Melina was bored and hungry. She wanted to help. She wanted to play. She even admitted to herself that she wanted to be good at it, not have Beau laugh or Rafe patronize her.

"Good practice, sport," Rafe said as they all walked to the parking lot, where Elliot's parents would pick him up.

"I didn't catch any fly balls," he said, kicking at the dirt.

"You will. It just takes practice. Tomorrow night

we'll work on that and on picking up grounders, okay?"

He nodded glumly.

"It was fun watching you hit," Melina said.

"That's easy."

"I'm a grown-up, and I can't do that."

"You're a girl."

Rafe laughed.

"Girls can hit balls, too, Elliot," Melina said, giving Rafe the eye so that he stifled his laughter. "We should watch one of the girls' games someday."

"There's only guys in the major leagues."

"Maybe it's time to change that," she said. "There are professional basketball leagues for women. And golf."

"Not football. It's hard. People get hurt a lot." He spotted his parents getting out of their car and took off running to them. "I hit a thousand!"

"I'm sorry for interfering with Beau," Rafe said to Melina as they followed Elliot more slowly. "He was being a jerk."

"What's new?"

"He's more of a jerk now than when we were in high school," Rafe said. "*Then* he was just relentless to get to the majors. *Now* he's fallen off the pedestal of success. It's a long fall, and a painful one."

They met up with Elliot and his parents and talked about how the practice went. "I told Elliot we'd work on fly balls and grounders tomorrow. We can't practice here, of course, but I'll figure out a place."

"Just let us know, and we'll be there," Steve Anderson said.

Elliot had climbed into the car and was buckling his seat belt. Rafe said quietly, "I think we need to keep it just him and me. He's responding well to my coaching. Would you mind?"

"Will you be there?" Steve asked Melina. "Please don't take this the wrong way, Rafe, but I don't know you yet. Today everything was out in public. Elliot's—"

"I'll be there," Melina said, interrupting, understanding a father's hesitation. She looked at Rafe. "We could use my parents' yard. It's plenty big."

A few beats passed. "Works for me," he said.

Melina heard reluctance in his voice, but the words were enough to satisfy a protective father.

"I'll email you the address," she said to Steve. "Or I can pick him up. You and Debbie talk it over and let me know. Maybe you two would like to go out to dinner or something. Have a date night. Elliot could eat dinner with us at my mom and dad's house after practice. My mom would be beyond thrilled to have him."

"Thank you, Melina. I'll let you know. He doesn't take to new people and situations easily, as you know," Steve said, then leaned close. "I think he's already a little more animated, don't you?"

"I do."

"He put on a hitting clinic," Rafe said, then cupped

Steve's shoulder. "You've done a great job teaching him."

"Thanks." The word came out as if causing him pain.

Melina and Rafe watched the family drive off then headed for her car. People were coming and going all around them, the parking lot a hive of activity.

"Want to practice with us tomorrow?" Rafe asked Melina after she unlocked her door.

"You mean you would deign to allow me to play, a mere girl?"

"I don't know about deigning, but I'd let you." His eyes sparkled. "Someone needs to run down the balls."

"Very funny. Would you like to stay for dinner after?" She hoped that sounded casual enough. If she was going to form a new kind of friendship with him, she needed to seem unaffected by him, even when he was smiling at her in that way that made her heart smile back.

"Maybe you'd better check with your parents first, Mel. I'm *persona non grata* with them, aren't I?"

"I can't see them saying no."

"Then, yes, thanks." He started to turn away. "Will Elliot be able to be independent someday? Live on his own?"

"He should. Many people with Asperger's have good and productive lives. You can't even imagine how much playing baseball is going to help him. It's a microcosm of the big world he'll face."

"Is there anything I should be doing differently with him?"

"Maybe talk to him when the opportunities come up about not hurting someone's feelings by what he says, not just once but every time something happens. Repetition is critical." She cocked her head. "You seem to be enjoying yourself."

"I've missed the game." He looked toward the fields. "You came to every one of my games. I could hear your voice over everyone else's."

"Are you calling me a loudmouth?"

"If the human megaphone fits…"

She gave him a playful sock on the shoulder, then they both laughed, something that hadn't happened since they'd met up again. It gave her hope that a friendship was in their future.

"Hey, Rafe! I heard you were back." A leggy red-head wearing skintight jeans and a low-cut, body-hugging T-shirt strode toward them, swiveling her hips as she walked. "Hello, Melina."

"June." Although she was dressed provocatively, June Adams was one half of the couple who'd been voted the second mostly likely to wed their senior year, and had. She and Wade had been married more than ten years and had two kids.

June gave Rafe a hug, flattening herself against him. He set his hands at her waist and eased her back. Melina frowned at the intimacy.

"How're you, June?" Rafe asked.

"Well, I'm doing fine, honey. Just fine. What're you doing dressed in your playing clothes?"

"Helping to coach one of the teams. What's new?" Rafe asked, giving her his full attention when she touched his arm, letting her hand slide down to his.

At the sexy gesture, Melina felt jealousy rise inside her. She wondered how her husband would feel if he was there to see June flirt so blatantly.

"I'm doing an article for the weekly on the start of baseball season. How 'bout I combine a couple of stories and write about you coming home *and* your return to baseball."

"Beau's your man. This is all his."

June maneuvered herself a little closer, putting herself between him and Melina.

"He was the story last year. This year we need a fresh angle."

Melina knew a story couldn't be written about Rafe's return to local baseball without including Elliot, and that would have to be cleared with his parents. She shook her head at Rafe.

"Not interested, thanks, June," he said. "Good to see you. Bye, Melina." He headed for his car.

June turned toward Melina. "Well, don't you look precious in your baseball cap."

Melina ignored the catty tone, unusual for June. While they'd never been really close, they'd always been friendly with each other. "How's Wade?" she asked.

June examined her fingernails then looked toward the horizon. "We split up."

"Oh, June. I'm so sorry. I hadn't heard." So much for the busy grapevine, Melina thought.

"You're the first person I've told, except for my parents. It just happened. I can't even say it was something in particular that ended it, but that it's been coming for a while. We just grew apart. I know it's a cliché, but it's the truth."

"Doesn't make it any easier."

"No. But I'll recover. The kids haven't fully grasped it yet. They're so little, you know? Anyway, I'm looking for a better job, so if you hear of anything, let me know, okay?"

"Sure." Melina hugged her. June leaned in for a second then pushed away and left, not looking back.

A bright light clicked on in Melina's brain as she watched June walk away, not with the swagger of earlier, but slowly, more carefully, as if afraid she would stumble. Melina saw a new truth then, not just clearly but in full-spectrum color—she and Rafe never would've found the happiness they'd expected because, in the end, they'd wanted different things. They'd been right for each other as teenagers, with teenage dreams and idealism, but they were adults now, settled in jobs they were passionate about, jobs that were so different from their original intent.

What if they'd gone ahead with their plans? Would they have been doomed to failure as time passed?

She had little doubt that their desire for each other wouldn't have changed, because that had been a constant. But a long-lasting relationship needed much more than great sex to survive.

They could've ended up like June and Wade, hurting, but also distressed for their children.

Melina headed to her car, trying to think ahead and how she would get through these next few weeks—months, really, since she had to attend the games, too, and sit in the dugout. Maybe being forced to work together would help her and Rafe become friends again so they wouldn't be uncomfortable when they ran into each other around town. Maybe they could start over, create something wholly different from the people they'd *become,* not who they'd been.

The true test would probably come when she saw him with another woman. Just that glimpse of him hugging June had fired up Melina. When he started dating someone and being together in public, that would be the true test.

She hoped it didn't happen before she was ready.

Chapter Seven

"You dropped more balls than I did," Elliot said seriously, factually, to Melina as they walked toward her parents' back door the next day after practice.

She shrugged and smiled. "I'm just learning. We did okay, though, didn't we, coach?"

"You did very well." Rafe could see Melina's mother, Patsy, through the kitchen window. She'd been watching and cooking for the past forty-five minutes. Melina's father wasn't home yet, but her grandfather was perched on the back porch and had been coaching from the sidelines, directing his comments at Melina.

"Let me see that mitt," Gramps said to her as she climbed the stairs. "Did you cinch it up with a belt last night like I told you?"

"Yes, sir, I did."

"Leave it with me for now. I'll work it a little more. You get a better pocket in it, you'll catch the ball more."

Rafe noticed that Elliot didn't look at her grandfather. Because of his gruffness? His age? His unfamiliarity? Not for the first time, Rafe wondered what it would be like to be in Elliot's head and see the world the way he did. He'd been excited about Rafe's trophies, and it had given them a connection they might not otherwise have had, but Rafe had to remember to be direct and specific with him. Elliot was more relaxed with Melina, but she wasn't new to him.

Rafe watched her toss her mitt and a ball to her grandfather then grip his shoulder and smile at him, getting a tender look in return. She'd always been like that—kind and caring, a toucher. She would've been a good lawyer, too, one who would've given her all for every client, every time. And she would've charged a sliding scale based on ability to pay, and done a lot of pro bono. At least, that had been her plan.

He considered his own achievements. He'd made a staggering amount of money for the few years he'd been in practice, but it hadn't come strictly from his profession. Mostly he'd let himself take huge risks by accepting a percentage in the businesses he represented instead of only a fee. Sometimes he lost, but mostly he won, selling his shares high, garnering great profits. It had given him a solid reputation in his field as well as the freedom to come back to Red Rock at a time when his father needed him.

Rafe followed Melina and Elliot into the house. She pointed out the bathroom to the boy, gave her mother a kiss on the cheek, then washed her hands at the kitchen sink.

"Thanks for having me, Patsy," Rafe said. "It smells great."

"Every once in a while you just have to have home-made fried chicken, I think," she said. "I invited your dad to join us."

Rafe couldn't hide his surprise. "Did he say yes?"

"He did. I've invited him several times since your mother died, but he's refused until now."

"He seems to be coming out of deep mourning finally," Rafe said.

"I think he's trying to, for your sake," Patsy said, lifting the last piece of chicken out of the cast-iron skillet, adding it to a platterful she was keeping warm in the oven. "You came home at the right time."

"Thanks." Rafe had always liked Patsy Lawrence, a feeling he knew used to be mutual. She was being polite but cautious with him now. Melina got her coloring from blonde and blue-eyed Patsy, although Patsy was willow slender, and her personality befitted the stereotype of a librarian, calm and knowledgeable.

"What can I do, Mom?" Melina asked.

"You can set the dining room table, please. Use the dark green tablecloth."

"I'll help. Let me wash up first," Rafe said, doing so, then going unerringly to the cabinet to get plates and glasses. He grabbed silverware from the drawer then went up beside Patsy.

"If my being here makes you uncomfortable, I won't come back again. I know Melina offered your house and yard without consulting you."

She smiled a little. "I admit it's strange after all these years, but...bygones, you know?"

Elliot came back and stood just inside the doorway, looking unsure.

"My daughter told me you love baseball," Patsy said. "I work at the library, and I saw a book there I thought you might like to read. It's on the kitchen table over there. Have you read it before?"

Elliot shook his head. He sat down to read. Rafe's hands full, he looked over Elliot's shoulder, seeing the book was baseball by the numbers—statistics of players and teams since the game began.

"Rafe Mendoza won't be in there," he said to the boy, smiling.

"You were good enough to play in the big leagues," Elliot said, not looking up from the book.

Elliot's comment struck a nerve that had laid dormant for years—until he'd gone to the field to speak to Beau the first time.

"Maybe. I had other plans," he said to Elliot, sensing Patsy's interest in their conversation.

He carried the place settings into the dining room, where Melina was folding napkins. As he set down the plates, déjà vu struck him. How many times had they done this, exactly this way? Too many to count. She'd been a constant visitor at his house, too.

"June and Wade Adams are separated," she said, looking up, connecting with his gaze. "She told me after you left. It came as a complete surprise to me. They always seemed fine whenever I saw them together."

"Remember their wedding?" Rafe said. He and Melina had gone together, just a few weeks after high school graduation. At the reception, they'd danced and dreamed out loud about their own future wedding. He'd never officially asked her to marry him, but he'd given her the promise ring, which meant he was promising to ask. He'd wanted to set a scene for that official proposal, something beautiful and memorable. If she wasn't going to be surprised by the question, she should be surprised at how he asked.

He remembered being happy that day, at Wade and June's wedding. His and Melina's lives were about to broaden immeasurably by going away to college and being independent. After dancing for a couple of hours, they'd driven to a hidden place by the river and made love, battling mosquitoes and laughing. Cherishing…

Then they'd sprawled, naked and satisfied, looking at each other, enjoying the sight. He hadn't dated anyone as curvy or as blonde as Melina since then—on purpose. No one who might remind him of her.

He wondered if she remembered that night in the same way. Then he saw her expression turn serious and her breath go shallow. She remembered, he decided, just as clearly as he, just as erotically. Her nipples were pressed against her snug T-shirt, then got visibly harder. So did he. And she noticed.

He moved around the table so that he could talk to her without being overheard. Barely any space separated them. "Why'd you kiss me the other night?" he asked.

"I couldn't help myself."

"What are we going to do about it?"

"It?"

He knew she couldn't be that obtuse. "You know, Melina. The attraction that never dies."

"It wasn't part of the plan I was formulating to only be friends with you," she said, moving a little closer, looking at his mouth. "Maybe it should be."

"Look who I found wandering outside," Melina's father bellowed from the kitchen, the back door hinges squeaking. "Can I get you a beer, Luis?"

Rafe's father's much softer voice didn't carry into the dining room, where Rafe and Melina jumped apart, caught like teenagers by their parents, and busied themselves setting the table so that by the time her father burst into the dining room, they no longer looked guilty.

"Hey, Dad," Melina said, going to give him a hug.

"How's my girl?" He patted her shoulder as she backed away. "Rafe."

"Sir." They shook hands, Rafe noting the suspicion in her father's eyes, the hesitance, but most of all the protectiveness.

His own father followed, a beer in hand. After greetings were exchanged, all the men wandered out to the back porch, taking Gramps a beer, as well.

Relief came over Melina once the door shut behind them. She wasn't sure what to expect putting that group of men together, but no fireworks so far.

She sat in a chair across from Elliot, who seemed comfortable being there, not fidgeting to leave. His parents had gone out for a rare dinner alone. Melina had hoped they wouldn't have to leave early and pick him up.

"Is Steph coming over, too?" she asked her mother.

"She's interviewing potential roommates now that Angie has moved in with Tommy. I think she's got three lined up for tonight. Would you grab the potato salad from the refrigerator, please? The rolls should be warmed enough, too. Green beans need to be put into a serving bowl."

Melina kept busy with the tasks but wondered if her mom wanted to ask questions and yet not be intrusive into her oldest daughter's life. After the food was taken care of, Melina rested an arm across her mother's shoulder and said, "We're doing this for Elliot."

Her mother smiled. "Are you?"

Melina nodded. "I figure by the time this is over, Rafe and I will be good friends, and I'll be glad about that."

"Your father's not happy about it at all."

"And you, Mom?"

"I see the hunger between you, Melina. I don't want you to suffer again."

The meal started awkwardly then smoothed out as time passed and conversation came more easily. Elliot kept his head down and ate well, including a big slice of pecan pie.

"Thank you for dinner, Patsy," Rafe's father said. "I haven't had chicken like that since..." He let the sentence drift off.

She laid her hand on the back of his. "It's Elena's recipe. She taught me how to fix it. I think of her all the time, but especially when I'm cooking certain dishes. She was the best cook I ever knew."

He nodded, looking down and swallowing hard, which brought tears to Melina's eyes.

"I miss her, too, Luis," Patsy said.

The whole table went quiet until Gramps said, "Did I tell you all that Melina thinks I should be dating?"

The conversation got lively again. Melina caught Rafe's gaze and smiled. It was such a familiar moment, all that laughter around the dining room table, although she felt the loss of her grandmother and Rafe's mother starkly.

The Andersons came to pick up Elliot, and the exodus began. Gramps yawned dramatically as his clue to Melina he wanted to go home. She couldn't manage a second alone with Rafe, but watched him go then drove her grandfather to his house.

After that she needed a swim. The day had been more cloudy than sunny, so the solar cover hadn't warmed the pool as much as it did on clear days.

Pent-up desire drove her lap after lap until finally she had to stop. She leaned her forehead against the side of the pool to catch her breath before she climbed out.

"Need a towel?"

The familiar voice didn't really surprise her. She'd been torn between wanting him to show up and wishing he would stay away.

She lifted her head. He was crouched, waiting for her, her towel held loosely in his hands, his eyes searching, questioning.

"Yes," she said in answer to everything and anything.

Then she climbed out of the pool and into his arms.

Chapter Eight

Melina had just barely shut her living room door when she found herself up against it, her hands locked with his, arms pressed to the painted wood. The towel dropped to the floor. Her bathing suit didn't create a barrier but friction instead, exciting and welcome, as he moved his body along hers.

"I'll only ask once," he said touching his forehead to hers, his face taut with desire. "Are you okay with this?"

She nodded, then his mouth was on hers, attacking at first, then slowing, lingering, indulging. Savoring. His fingers tightened and released around hers, again and again, mimicking what was to come. He let go, freeing his hands to touch her, to slide his palms down her back and over her rear, cupping her, bringing her even closer as he dragged his mouth down her neck. Her wet hair dripped onto him and the floor. The scent of chlorine made her wish for a shower, but she didn't want to wait that long. Couldn't wait. This moment had been building, day by day. She needed him here and now.

Melina curved her fingers into his flesh as he sank slowly, exhaling hot air through her suit as he made a meandering trail down her welcoming body, stopping to nibble here and there, to run his hands along her breasts, her abdomen and beyond. She arched as his mouth settled between her legs, his fiery breath arousing, his teeth finding just the right places with just the right pressure. Then he rose, bringing along her towel to rub her hair, drawing audible breaths, deep and shaky.

She took him by the hand and led him upstairs and into her bedroom, wishing she knew what to say, wanting words from him, as well. And yet, what would they say?

He moved past her, flipped on two bedside lights, grabbed hold of her bedding and pulled it down, leaving only the bottom sheet. When he faced her he seemed like an entirely different person from her memories of him—a fully adult male instead of a young man, one who had life experience now. Other sexual experiences. She wondered—

"Take off your suit," he said, low and harsh, standing two feet from her.

She hesitated only long enough for the order to

reach her brain, then peeled it off and tossed it toward her bathroom, where it landed with a splat.

Then he stripped, all the while watching her, revealing his perfectly toned body slowly, enticingly. She wanted to feel him inside her right now....

"I'm on the pill," she said, reaching toward him, needing to touch, to feel, to taste. He would be familiar and yet new. The memory of this night would replace others from so long ago. Was that a good thing? She would know soon.

She started at his chest, teasing him with light touches, exploring the planes of his body, going lower and lower, until he sucked in an audible breath. She wrapped her hand around his bold heat, swirled a fingertip around and around, glorying in the sounds he made.

"Keep it up and I won't be of much use to you," he said through clenched teeth.

"Oh, I fully intend to keep it up."

His laugh was filled with frustration and arousal. He let her explore for a little longer, then he took charge, moving her onto the bed, landing on top of her, maneuvering his legs between hers to nestle heat to heat, capturing her mouth with his in a deep, hot kiss that shut out the world, encasing them in their own erotic cocoon. She wrapped her legs around him, felt the hard heat of him press against her, pressure building inside her from the contact alone....

Rafe felt her arch and clench, heard her breathless sounds, squeezed his eyes shut when her fingernails dug into him and she moved rhythmically, power-fully. The moment she started to slow, he slid down her, took a hard nipple in his mouth and cherished it, then the other, arousing her again, ready to explode himself. His hands moved over her warm flesh, his mouth tasted her skin until he threaded his fingers through the soft curls between her legs—and then let his mouth go exploring.

He didn't have to wait for a response. She cupped his head, grabbed his hair, angled her hips higher. She was vocal and bold in her pleasure, then demand-ing as she pulled him up until he buried himself in-side her, feeling her envelop him and tighten, finding paradise and satisfaction and a need for much, much more.

After a couple of minutes, Melina reached for the sheet to drag over them. Rafe had dropped onto his back, breathing hard, his arm across his eyes.

While she waited for him to say something, she looked around. Her bedroom was simple, the bed itself decorated with a white matelasse coverlet, a sage green dust ruffle and a few contrasting pillows—which had been tossed onto the floor in the heat of passion. Her pine furniture was bought at a yard sale and refin-ished. The real color came from family photos on the dresser and some of her mother's stunning art on the walls, single flowers in deep, rich tones, their bold colors at odds with her mother's calm, soothing personality.

What are you thinking? she asked Rafe silently. Maybe he'd fallen asleep. Or maybe he was avoiding talking to her. For all the heat between them, it had also been comfortable. No awkwardness of a first time, even though he had some moves that were new to her. Did he want to spend the night? Continue the relationship after this?

Or would this be it?

Finally he stirred, letting his arm fall away from his face. He opened his eyes and met her gaze, his expression serious. "We haven't lost our touch," he said.

Which told her nothing. "No."

He watched her a while longer. "Do you want me to go?"

Her stomach clenched. Her throat burned, tears threatening. He didn't even want to hold her for a while? "It's up to you, Rafe."

In truth she didn't know if she wanted him to go or stay. What could they talk about? To only discuss casual topics like Elliot or Beau or their families would dilute the intensity of their lovemaking, driven by a desire left unresolved for too long.

And yet, she felt good, too. He'd wanted her as much as she'd wanted him. Time and distance had only strengthened their physical compatibility.

She'd spent years keeping her relationships short and simple. If she could do that with Rafe, would it run its course by the end of baseball season, so that they could go their separate ways, the past buried, the future brighter for both of them?

"I'd be lying if I said I didn't want more." Rafe rolled to his side, facing her. "But I don't want to overstay my welcome."

"Your decision."

"No, it isn't. Yes or no, Melina? Go or stay?"

She decided she didn't want him to stay, that she didn't want to talk or hang out watching television or whatever other possibilities there were, since it was several hours until bedtime.

"If you leave, is that it for us?" she asked.

"Meaning what? You want to keep me as your stud?"

"Something like that." Her heart pounded so loud she thought surely he would hear it. She'd intended to be friends with him, not lovers, but maybe answering the attraction would help seal their future relationship. "I'm not seeing anyone right now," she said.

"Nor am I." He tucked her hair—her still-damp, totally messed-up hair—behind her ear then rubbed her lobe. "I'm game. So. How does this work?"

"We meet every so often for sex, but we won't spend the night." She didn't know why, but sleeping with him seemed more intimate than having sex with him.

"Well, now, that's a fascinating proposition, Mel. I'm to be your boy toy when the need arises, but that's all? We won't have dinner together or watch a movie? Sex only, no strings attached?"

She wanted strings. She wanted nights in his arms and waking up to watch the sunrise and a kiss good-bye in the morning. She *didn't* want her parents finding out and the reproachful looks that would follow, or the pity when it ended. Because it *would* end—she had no doubt about that.

"Yes, that's exactly what I want," she said, sure of her decision finally.

"And either of us can end it when we see fit, no recriminations, no blame? A no-fault affair, as it were?"

"We're adults. We can choose what kind of relationship we want." But even as she said the words, she knew it wasn't true. She was already falling in love with him again. If she'd ever stopped loving him.

He didn't speak for at least thirty seconds. Feeling almost sick to her stomach, she waited and waited.

"Okay," he said at last.

She wanted to weep. It was what she'd wanted to hear, and yet it wasn't enough.

"Have you been happy, Rafe?" she asked.

"Yes."

"Life is what you expected?" she asked, wanting more of an answer.

"More than I expected."

"Yet you moved back here…"

"I've made a whole lot of money, and that's not going to stop because I live here now. I have a certain skill that people pay well for, and an above-average tolerance for risk. I won't apologize for what I've achieved. It feels good."

"Do you ever wish you'd taken a shot at the big leagues?"

"Now and then."

They climbed out of bed. He took her hand and pulled her toward the bathroom.

They didn't have much to say after that, just let their shower-wet kisses and soapy hands do all the talking. By the time he left an hour later, her body ached contentedly and her heart discontentedly. She'd entered into an arrangement that could lead either to a purging of past blame and hurt or a whole new level of agony.

Either way, she had to give it a shot, once and for all. Her peace of mind depended on it.

Rafe hadn't been home for two minutes when someone knocked on his front door.

Melina's father stood in the doorway. Rafe didn't invite him in, nor did he address the man. He'd always called Melina's mother Patsy, but he had never called her father Jefferson—or even Mr. Lawrence. Just *Sir*.

"I want you to leave my daughter alone. And before you say anything—I know you've been at her place for the past two hours."

"You also know we're working together on Elliot Anderson's situation."

Jefferson's gaze pierced him. His hands fisted.

"My girl went through hell after you walked away. She's been steady on her feet for a while now. She doesn't need tripping up by you again."

Rafe clamped his mouth against the words that threatened to spill. *He'd* walked away? Like hell he had. The fact that Jefferson didn't know the truth made Rafe wonder if everyone thought the same— that Rafe had ended the relationship, when it wasn't true at all. He'd *acknowledged* the end, but *that* was it.

All Rafe said to her father, however, was, "Message received, sir."

The vague response obviously didn't please Jefferson. "You know, son, I did some checking on you. You were a real ladies man in Ann Arbor, weren't you? Cut a wide swath."

"So?" He'd had no reason not to. To his knowledge he hadn't broken any hearts.

"Melina's a good girl. She deserves to find a man to marry and bear his children. She won't do that if you keep stringing her along."

Rafe almost laughed. If only Jefferson knew the deal Melina had just presented Rafe with. Who was stringing whom along? Rafe did, on the other hand, understand a father's love.

"As I said, sir. Message received." It was all he could promise, after all. It was Melina's choice as much as his.

"I'll be keeping an eye on you," Jefferson said,

then he stalked silently down the front path to his big pickup truck and rumbled away.

Rafe shut the door but didn't move. He shouldn't feel guilty, but he did. He'd done nothing wrong, yet apparently he was the bad guy in the breakup scenario. If that were the case, why had Melina let him back into her life? *He* was the one who should be leery.

After all, she was the one who'd broken his heart.

Chapter Nine

Red hadn't yet hit its Friday-night stride when Rafe met up with Ross Fortune and orthopedic surgeon Jeremy Fortune for an early dinner. Marcos had given them a corner booth, announcing that Wendy Fortune would be their server, then winking at Rafe as he did so, as if to say, "You'll see what an experienced server she is."

"Howdy cousins," she said, eyeing the two Fortune men thoughtfully. "You all look like nachos and beer fans. A pitcher of light, and a big plate of extra-peppers nachos coming up."

The men had looked at each other and smiled. "Summed us up pretty well, I think," Rafe said, getting nods in return.

"I hear congratulations are in order," Rafe said to

Jeremy. "Seems you've gotten yourself engaged since we last spoke in my office a couple weeks ago."

"Thanks. I'm feeling pretty lucky these days. Maybe you'd like to come to dinner one night and meet Kirsten? Are you seeing anyone these days, Rafe? Someone you'd like to bring along?"

"I'd like to meet your fiancée, and no, I'm not seeing anyone."

"That's not what the word on the internet is," Ross said.

"Huh?" was all Rafe could manage.

"You and Melina Lawrence have been linked."

"On the *internet?*"

"June's 'Around Town' column for the newspaper. It's on the paper's website as a daily column before it hits the stands in print." The often-gruff, dark-haired P.I. seemed to be enjoying himself at Rafe's expense.

Rafe stopped talking as Wendy set down a pitcher and three frosty glasses.

"Nachos'll be up in a minute," she said, walking away with purpose, hips twitching, which slowed the men's conversation for a few seconds.

"It's a rumor," Rafe finally said to Ross, "based on nothing more than Melina's and my proximity on a couple of occasions. Purely speculation."

"Speak of the devil," Ross said as Marcos led Melina, her sister Stephanie and Q into the dining room, seating them in direct view of the men, although not within hearing distance.

Stephanie waved but didn't shout out a greeting the way her sister Angie would have. Still, it was enough for Melina to notice. She followed Stephanie's gaze then tentatively lifted a hand. Was she blushing? It was hard to tell from this distance, but Rafe thought her cheeks had gone rosy. Was she remembering the night before, especially what had happened in the shower? Or was she a little embarrassed, perhaps? Maybe she'd read June's rumors online and was being teased by her companions, just as he was.

"Is that the famous Melina?" Jeremy asked. "I haven't met her."

"The blonde is Melina," Rafe said. "The redhead is her sister Stephanie. The alpha male goes by Q. He's Melina's business partner." Rafe looked at Jeremy, changing the subject. "Still no word on your father?"

"Nothing," Jeremy said, shaking his head. "He's been missing for three months now, but I can't shake the feeling that he's out there somewhere."

Rafe exchanged a glance with Ross. "He could very well be right," Ross said. "William's car was found, but not his body. He was supposed to get married the day he disappeared, and there was no reason for him to run away. I haven't turned up anything."

"And the police have given up," Jeremy added, frustration in his voice. "And now there's this baby, who mysteriously appears the same day that my father goes missing—at the same church, no less. We can't find any connection to the two events, but it's an odd coincidence, don't you think?"

"Here's your nachos, gentlemen," Wendy said. She was bright and perky without being obnoxious. "Y'all ready to order? Or do you want to hold off awhile?"

Rafe couldn't figure why Marcos thought Wendy wasn't a good waitress. So far, she was great, letting them enjoy their drinks and appetizer before ordering dinner, if that was their choice. She was cute, friendly without being over-the-top. The job suited her well.

The three men ordered their meals then returned to their discussion. Baby Anthony's fate was up in the air, except that Jeremy and Kirsten were prepared to give him up to the child's natural parents, if and when they were found.

"We thought Kirsten's brother, Max, was the baby's father, because that was what this girl, Courtney, told him," Jeremy said. "But that was apparently a lie. Then Courtney changed her story and said that a guy named Charlie is the baby's father, not Max, and that Charlie is bad news. So, Kirsten and I are acting as court-appointed guardians for the moment, because another big revelation followed—Courtney admitted she's not the mother. And then she gave Max the medallion the baby was wearing—"

"What medallion?" Ross interrupted, just as Rafe was going to ask for replay of the complicated story. "What are you talking about?"

"Baby Anthony apparently had on a small gold

medallion when he was found in the car seat at the church. Or so the story goes."

"This is the first I'm hearing about it," Ross said.

"Because Courtney just turned it over, but she's also lied so much that no one knew—or knows—what to believe. Is she just trying to confuse everyone? Is she playing a game? If so, why?"

"Where is the medallion?" Ross asked.

"At home."

"I need to see it."

"It's just a trinket, Ross, but I can call Kirsten and have her bring it by. She and the baby are meeting a friend of Kirsten's shortly since I wasn't going to be home for dinner."

"If it's not too much trouble. Or I can go home with you after dinner."

"Not at all. I'll have her text me when she gets here so she doesn't have to get Anthony out of the car." He pulled out his phone.

Rafe had been half listening, his thoughts drifting elsewhere, like to last night in Melina's bed…and shower.

"I'd say June's 'Around Town' rumors are fact," Ross said, leaning close. "Or you want them to be true, at least."

"We have a past."

"A legendary one." Ross stood. "I'll be back in a minute."

Rafe winced. He wondered if Melina was hearing

the same rumors and taking a lot of teasing. He pulled out his phone and sent a text message to her: "Free later?"

He watched her pick up her phone and look at it, then over at him. She could've nodded or shaken her head but instead texted back an answer: "Not free, but reasonable."

He smiled at her, then wrote, "Eight? Your place?"

"Don't be late," she wrote back.

"Kirsten's on her way," Jeremy said. "I'm going out front to wait for her. Don't eat all the nachos."

Which left Rafe alone at the table. He made his way across the dining room to say hello.

"We're celebrating my last day at the office," Stephanie said. "Angie will be back to work on Monday."

"We're celebrating a *successful* week," Q added. "Stephanie filled in admirably."

"And I didn't reorganize the file cabinets or anything." She grinned. "I did change Angie's desk around a little, just to mess with her."

"You wouldn't be a good sister otherwise," Rafe said.

"Have you been abandoned?" Melina asked.

"No. They'll be back. I just wanted to say hi." He started to walk away, then turned back. "Apparently we are the subject of public gossip," he said to Melina.

"You are the hundredth person to tell me that—or thereabouts."

He couldn't read her expression. Did it bother her? "I'd contact June and demand a retraction, except I think it might add fuel to the fire."

"It'll die on its own without that fuel," Melina said casually.

"Or not," Stephanie said with a smirk. Her eyes sparkled as she sipped her margarita.

Rafe excused himself, happy to get away from the curiosity in Stephanie's eyes as Ross and Jeremy returned to the booth.

Wendy brought their dinners just as they all took their seats. "Anything else I can get you?" she asked.

"We're good," Rafe said.

As soon as she left the dining room, the three men traded plates. She hadn't gotten one right. They all smiled and shrugged. So, she got their orders mixed up. She'd still get a great tip, Rafe thought. What she lacked in skill, she more than made up for in amiability.

Jeremy passed a plastic baggie to Ross. Inside was a small gold medallion on a chain. Ross stared at it, then set down his fork, opened the bag and dumped the item into his palm. The chain was delicate but the medallion itself looked like an old coin of some sort.

"Something wrong?" Rafe asked when Ross remained silent.

"I don't know. There's something about it. It's ringing a bell, but I don't know why. Obviously it has significance if it came with the baby. Can I hold on to this, Jeremy? I need to research it, if I can."

"Kirsten and I have tried, believe me, and came up empty. Have at it, Ross. I take it you didn't come up with any clues from the baby's car seat?"

He shook his head. "The brand is sold in every Walmart in the country."

"May I see the necklace?" Rafe asked.

Ross set it in Rafe's palm. "Did you have it appraised?" he asked Jeremy. "Is it gold? If it's a trinket it may be hard to track down its origins, but if it's gold…"

He passed it back to Ross, who frowned thoughtfully at it, then dropped it back into the baggie then into his pocket.

"No, we didn't have it appraised," Jeremy said. "We tried to find a match on the internet, but that's all. We haven't had possession of it for very long."

"I know some dealers," Ross said, picking up his fork. "The image is really resonating with me, though, so maybe it won't be that hard to track down. I must've seen it at some point."

The men spoke of other things then, including how much Red Rock had changed since they were kids. Although Ross was forty-two and Jeremy thirty-seven, Rafe had heard about them all his life—all the Fortunes, actually. They were like royalty in this area. Rafe felt on an equal footing with them, all of them professional and successful.

Marcos came up to ask how their meal was, and then the all-important question about how their service was. Gentlemen to the end, none of them mentioned Wendy's error. Rafe figured she'd get it worked out on her own when less polite customers pointed out her mistakes.

Ross and Jeremy took off after dinner. Q left, as well, leaving Melina and Stephanie alone. Rafe stood, figuring he'd join them, but another young woman came along and slid into the booth with them. Stephanie introduced her to Melina, then they called Wendy over and ordered something.

Rafe was at a loss. He couldn't go to Melina's house for another hour. He didn't want to go home. Just then Marcos came back to the table, their father behind him.

"I know you've already eaten," Luis said. "But maybe you have time to keep me company while I have dinner?"

"Of course, Dad. I've got about an hour before I meet someone. Plenty of time."

His father had just gotten settled when Beau Bandero showed up—with June Adams. Rafe didn't think there were two people in town he wanted to see less. He knew, however, he needed to be polite to both of them.

"Evening, June. Beau," Rafe said as Marcos started to walk past Rafe's table.

"Where're you putting us?" Beau asked Marcos, who gestured toward a corner booth. "Okay, we'll seat ourselves in a minute. Mr. Mendoza, how're you?" he said to Rafe's father.

Rafe saw an entirely different Beau at that moment, respectful and genuinely happy to see Luis, shaking his hand and smiling, engaging him in conversation.

Rafe glanced at June. "I was sorry to hear about you and Wade."

She shrugged. "Been coming awhile."

"Still, it's hard. Especially on the kids." Rafe shot Beau a look, but he seemed immersed in his conversation. "You going out with him?"

Her brows lifted high. "I'm interviewing him, as you suggested. He offered to buy dinner. I don't turn down free dinners. Money's a little scarce these days."

"So it won't show up in your column, I guess. Who's in charge of writing speculation about *you,* June?"

She cocked her head. "You mad about that, Rafe?"

"I'm part of a dying breed, I think, of people who believe in an expectation of having a certain amount of privacy in our lives. And truth."

"I write what I see. If I don't see it myself, I verify what information I'm given."

"You ready?" Beau asked June, who nodded a goodbye then preceded him to their booth.

Rafe's back was to them, which was just as well. He eyed Melina, saw her watching them.

Something to talk about later.

"You and Beau get all caught up?" Rafe asked his father, not doing a good job of hiding his irritation. Beau had always admired Luis, had come to him for advice when Beau and Rafe were teenagers. Rafe had always felt it was a betrayal of some kind that his father had counseled Rafe's rival.

Taquitos and guacamole had been delivered to the table without Rafe seeing it happen. Even though he wasn't hungry, he snatched one up, dipped it in the guac, took a bite as his father sat back and eyed his son casually.

"Yes, thank you. We did. And you have no reason to be jealous."

"Jealous? I'm not—" He clamped his mouth shut. "Yes, I am. You always seemed so much more patient with him than me."

"I was responsible for how *you* turned out, son. Beau needed a strong male influence. He found it in me. Being ranch foreman, I was usually around."

"His father is about the strongest man out there."

"Hard's a better word for him. And he was too hard on Beau. Don't you remember at your games how he'd chew Beau out from the stands? Embarrass him?"

After a moment, Rafe nodded. "Do you think

that's why he has the no-parents-allowed rule at practices?"

"No question. He'd probably ban them from the games, too, if he could." Luis took a sip of beer then set his glass down carefully. "It's probably difficult for you to see this, since you were going to succeed whether you decided to try for the big leagues or become a lawyer—but Beau only had one chance. The only thing he was good at was baseball. Mr. Bandero finally showed some pride in his son when the Astros signed Beau. Then he got injured, ending his career. And now you're rubbing your success in his face just by coming back here—not because you're doing anything in particular, but because that's who *he* is. He doesn't feel worthy. His father never inspired that in him. Just the opposite, in fact. Beau has to succeed now or else."

Rafe considered the long-winded argument. His father didn't often speak so emotionally, so it obviously meant a lot to him that Rafe understand Beau's situation. "He was never an easy guy to be around, Dad, but I can see that he has to put out winners now in order to prove he isn't washed up at twenty-nine. But surely you know that I don't kick a man while he's down."

His father patted his arm.

"How are you doing?" Rafe asked, changing the subject. "Except for dinner at Melina's last night, you've made yourself scarce."

"I guess she was right when she said I needed to

tell you how I was feeling. I've been sleeping better in my own bed." He dipped a taquito into the guac and examined it as he said casually, "I accepted Patsy's invitation last night because I was wondering if something was going on between you and Melina, even though you've said it's just business. You avoided looking at each other so much, I decided there *is* something going on."

Rafe almost laughed. Apparently, they couldn't look at each other, and they couldn't *not* look at each other. Both led to suspicion.

"No response?" Luis asked in surprise.

"I don't know what to say." Rafe glanced at Melina, who was laughing with her sister and the other woman. "We've both grown up and changed. We are making a point of getting along so that Elliot can have a shot at playing ball on a team. Melina and I probably would've avoided each other, if not for that. I'm glad we got forced to work together. Everything is okay." And in less than an hour, they would be in bed together proving just how okay they were.

Rafe left his father at the restaurant ten minutes before eight. Melina had taken off a half hour earlier after stopping by Beau and June's table then Rafe and his father's to say goodbye.

Rafe knew he had to move his car from the restaurant parking lot or June might have another news item to leak, but he didn't want to leave it in the guest parking spaces for Melina's building, either. In the end he parked on a side street and walked to her townhouse.

When she opened her door, she greeted him wearing a floor-length, lacy black negligee showing off her tempting cleavage. Red-painted toenails peeped out from below the frilly hem.

She didn't look shy or hesitant or restrained, and he found her confidence incredibly sexy.

But a couple of hours later as he walked back to his car, he found himself feeling dissatisfied, a feeling that carried over whenever they got together during the next week. During their brief time together each evening, they talked less and less, making love passionately, but in silence, and with little laughter.

When they were done, he would leave her bed, dress in the dark and let himself out into the cold, dreary night, finding less contentment each time, and yet, oddly, wanting her more, wishing she would talk to him the way she used to, wishing they could have breakfast together to start their days.

Since his return to town, he'd seen endless patience in her—with other people. With him, she never relaxed, never let him linger, never let him just hold her tucked close to him.

It didn't bode well for when baseball season ended.

Chapter Ten

"You've lost weight," Angie commented when Melina arrived at work on a Tuesday afternoon over a week later.

"No, I haven't," Melina said, picking up her message slips from the corner of Angie's desk.

Angie stared coolly at her sister.

"Okay, maybe a couple of pounds," Melina conceded, although she knew it was closer to five, maybe more. "I've been busy. Between seeing patients and helping with Elliot's practice almost every evening, I'm always on the go."

"And you forget to eat?"

"I eat. Sporadically. Anyway, I could stand to lose a few pounds."

"You look great, Mellie, especially since you started swimming. This is about Rafe, isn't it?"

Melina pretended to read her messages but was really counting to ten. "Why would it be about Rafe?"

"Women lose weight either *for* a man or because of one. Or for her wedding," she added, holding her arms out, showing off her wedding-perfect figure, fifteen pounds lighter than when she got engaged. With her honeymoon tan not having faded yet, she was a knockout, but Melina thought it was Angie's inner happiness showing through.

"I'm just busy," Melina said firmly, then headed into her office, shutting her door, ending the discussion. Of course it was about Rafe. Keeping him close while also keeping him at a distance was taking its toll on her. She wanted to curl up in bed with him after they made love, to talk about things she didn't usually share with anyone, but he'd made it clear he was there only for the sex.

Every time he came over, the scenario was the same—they made love with wild abandon, their hands and bodies and mouths in constant motion, giving and taking as if it were the last time. They would shower after and arouse each other to the point of no return, then go to bed again and make love much more slowly and tenderly.

Then he would stretch out on his back with his eyes closed for a minute. After that he would roll out of bed, get dressed, give her a short, soft kiss and leave.

He showed up every night at the same time, left at the same time. The two hours in between were exciting, and yet...

And yet she was restless. He seemed fine with the arrangement, didn't seem to want to take it beyond what it already was.

Melina sat at her desk and stared at a painting of an endless field of bluebonnets her mother had painted as an office-warming gift.

You're the one who set the parameters, she reminded herself. But he was a hot-blooded man with a mind and will of his own, and if he wanted to change the rules, he could, or at least try.

In fact, she would welcome it, because she'd spent enough time with him both in bed and at the ballpark to have taken that dangerous, irresponsible step of falling in love with him again, especially after watching him with Elliot day after day.

Rafe had endless patience with the boy. There had been no need for Melina's presence, because Rafe knew how to divert Elliot when he got frustrated and settle him down to focus on practicing again. Elliot expected perfection of himself. Rafe let him know it would never be possible.

There were only nine more days until the first official game. Eight days until the final team practice, when Beau said he would decide if Elliot would go or stay. Melina didn't know who would be more upset if Beau wouldn't keep him—Elliot or Rafe. Or what the end result would be.

Would Rafe have a legal avenue to pursue for Elliot? And what kind of life lesson would it be for Elliot if he'd tried his hardest and been denied the opportunity to play? He hadn't been told of the possibility of not playing with the team. Maybe he should be warned.

Melina shoved her hair back from her face and blew out a breath. She couldn't think about it right now. She'd worked with four patients today and needed to enter notes into their files. She opened Big John's first. He'd had a stroke three months ago and had a staff of therapists—physical, speech and occupational. She'd retaught him how to make scrambled eggs today and bowled with him using a Wii. He was only sixty-two and wanted to drive his truck again, to get back to work at his job as an electrician. He was working hard toward that goal but was ornery as all get-out.

Melina had also worked that day with Elliot and a girl named Cindi in their classrooms at school. And then there was sweet Deenie, who was eighty, had no family nearby and was trying to live alone after hip replacement. Her daily, uncomplaining perseverance usually brought Melina to tears. She'd rearranged furniture and cabinet contents so that Deenie could maneuver easily around her tiny house, but everything was a struggle for her, with only slight improvement day by day. Melina checked in on her more often than she was scheduled for or paid to, because she worried about the frail woman.

A knock on Melina's office door startled her. Angie stuck her head inside. "I'm heading home. And Rafe's here to see you." She waggled her eyebrows and grinned.

"See you tomorrow, Ang. Please tell him to come in." She looked at her watch, surprised to see it was only twenty minutes until practice started. She backed up her data then shut off her computer as Rafe walked in, leaving the door open.

Melina didn't get up to greet him. She didn't know the etiquette in this situation. They were secret lovers. Did that mean they should hug hello as friends might? No, she decided, even though they were alone in the office.

"Hey," she said as he stood just inside the doorway. "Have a seat."

"I just need a minute. I wanted to let you know that I can't come over tonight. Wasn't sure if we would have a moment alone at practice to tell you."

She waited for him to say why, but he didn't. "Okay. Thanks for letting me know."

He hesitated a moment longer then turned away. "See you at practice."

Melina didn't move until she heard the front door close. He could have sent her a text message telling her, but he'd chosen to come in person. Why? He also could've chosen to tell her why he wouldn't be coming, but he hadn't done that either. Why not?

This was Tuesday, an unusual day for a date, if that was what he was up to—and the reason he wasn't giving.

By the time she reached the ballpark, she was thoroughly annoyed. She was good enough to sleep with but not to confide in or be open with?

Are you open with him? her conscience asked, chiding her.

Well, no. Not completely.

So, whose fault is that?

Okay, okay, okay. She got it. By trying to keep herself from getting involved emotionally, she'd created an environment where her emotions were tested all the time. Oh, for the simple days of high school and pure, uncomplicated love.

When she got to the field, she waved at Elliot then sat in the dugout and watched the sky darken. The air smelled of impending rain, although it wasn't forecast until the overnight hours.

Melina spotted June Adams's sexy stride from across the field. The black tote she carried was too bulky to be a purse, so Melina guessed it was a camera bag and that June was here in an official capacity for the newspaper.

She popped into the dugout. "Hey, Melina. Mind if I leave my bag here while I take a few shots of the kids?"

One of Elliot's quirks was that he didn't like his picture taken, but Melina didn't want to explain that to June, who might see Elliot as newsworthy. He wanted to fit in, not stand out.

"June," Melina said, "I'm going to ask a favor of you—that you take pictures on any other diamond." It wouldn't matter if the camera was aimed at the other kids on his team, Elliot would react to it, believing it was on him, although, contradicting all that, he really wanted a team photo, craved that. When it was his choice and he was prepared for the photograph, he was okay with it.

June frowned. "I want to shoot Beau's team. The article's about him."

"He coaches another set of kids right after this one."

"I can't hang around that long. I've got kids to get home to and feed." She slipped her camera strap over her head. "What's the big deal? Beau said I could come today."

Melina fired a look at Beau, who looked back—or maybe he was looking at June. Melina had prepared him for Elliot's behaviors, how sometimes he calmed his own anxiety by rocking his body rhythmically, that he often needed to line things up in a row—his baseball gear, for example—but the photo taking hadn't occurred to her.

She could ask Elliot, but it would interrupt practice to do so, and they weren't wearing uniforms yet because the season hadn't started, so she thought he might object, even if asked. So far he hadn't had any outbursts in front of his teammates, and Melina hoped it would stay that way, for his sake. Acceptance was something he was looking forward to, part of being on a team. It was as much a goal for him as learning to play.

"Could you hold off for just a minute, please," Melina said to June, then jogged over to where Rafe stood next to Elliot, who was taking grounders from one of the coaches. She explained the situation.

"I'll talk to June," he said. "Stay with Elliot."

"Where's he going?" Elliot asked right away, not even seeing the ball coming at him so that it scooted past.

"To talk to the lady in the dugout for a second. He'll be back. Just go ahead and play, Elliot. Everything's fine."

"I need him. I don't know how to do this."

She heard anxiety building in his voice, fear in his eyes. "I'll be right here, I promise."

"I need Rafe Mendoza."

Normally Melina would've taken him aside and talked to him, but she was trying not to make a big deal in front of his teammates. As a matter of course, he got enough teasing at school. He'd learned to deal with that, but his teammates were different. He wanted their acceptance. "He'll be right back. Coach Greg is waiting on you, Elliot. Keep practicing."

Melina knew Elliot and Rafe had gotten close in the past couple of weeks, but the depth of Elliot's dependency startled her. She walked over to stand right next to him. "I'm here with you, and Rafe just has to talk to the lady for a minute." She didn't want to pull Elliot off the field, but she could see he was determined not to be apart from Rafe.

"How about if we walk over there together?" she said to him quietly. "Slowly, okay? Don't run. I bet he'll be on his way back before we get there."

Melina felt people starting to stare, including Beau. The kids had a vague understanding that Elliot was new to playing baseball and needed more help, and since their goal was to win, they'd accepted Rafe being his personal coach. But to pull Elliot out of practice was another thing altogether.

She pleaded silently with Beau, who ordered the kids to give him their attention. Some did, some continued to watch Elliot, noting how he'd started running. Thunder rolled in the distance. He called Rafe's name.

Rafe came out to meet him, shifting his glance to Melina momentarily. "Hey, sport. What's going on?"

"I need you."

"I'm here." He turned to June. "Are we okay?"

She nodded.

Just then the skies opened up and rain came down hard.

"Everyone in the dugout," Beau shouted.

Because they were only a few feet away, Rafe, Elliot, Melina and June ducked inside the covered structure first. Melina watched the other kids eye Elliot, but he didn't look at them in return, so he didn't see the curiosity and, from a few of the kids, the ridicule in their expressions. One mouthed "Baby" to another, who smirked.

She decided to talk to Elliot's parents. Explaining the situation to his teammates might help. Then again, she wouldn't blame his parents if they decided against it, since he would feel even more different. At this age, it was tough to make that kind of call.

Beau talked skills as the rain poured down noisily. Elliot sat on the bench and rocked. Eventually his actions slowed and he seemed to be paying attention again. Melina and his parents had been working with him on apologizing, on understanding the importance of doing so, but he hadn't grasped the concept routinely. But out of the blue he said, "I'm sorry for walking off."

To Beau's credit, he didn't push Elliot to say why. "Thank you, Elliot. We accept your apology, don't we, boys?"

Everyone nodded or shifted or made some kind of sound. Melina tried to thank Beau with her eyes, but his hardened, as if to say, "This isn't the end of this."

They all stayed in the dugout listening to Beau's lecture until practice time ended, then they raced to the parking lot to catch their rides home. Melina decided to call the Andersons later rather than try to talk to them in the rain. She wondered if Elliot would be quieter than usual, making them wonder what had happened.

Rafe and Melina hunched under an eave, waiting for traffic to thin before they went to their cars.

"You probably don't know it, but that was a big step for Elliot, apologizing like that, without anyone telling him to," she said to Rafe.

A few beats passed. "I told him to. I whispered it in his ear. I shouldn't have?"

"Oh." The wind went out of her sails for a moment. "No, it's okay. I was just excited because— Well, it's good that you reinforced that behavior. Thanks."

"What was going on with him?"

"He panicked when you walked away. I'm a little worried about the level of attachment he has with you, Rafe. What happens if you can't make it for a practice or game sometime? Maybe I need to be more involved so that he would adapt to having me work with him, just in case."

"I'll talk to Beau about it."

"What'd you say to June, anyway?"

"I appealed to the mom in her. She won't take pictures or do any kind of story without talking to the Andersons." He looked at the sky. "Looks like it's not going to let up. I should get going."

He'd barely looked at her, and kept himself more than a foot away. Worst of all, he seemed in a hurry to get away.

"Why aren't you coming to my place tonight?" she asked, unable not to.

He finally focused on her. "I have a meeting with Ross Fortune. Will you miss me?"

"Yes."

He closed his eyes for a few seconds. When he opened them, his expression was entirely different. She saw tenderness and a building desire, his eyes darkening by the second. "That's what I've been waiting to hear," he said, his voice low.

"Did you think it doesn't matter to me whether I see you?"

"We never talk, Mel. We have sex—great sex—but that's it. I don't know how you feel about anything."

"I thought it was what you wanted."

"I thought it was what *you* wanted." He inched a little closer. "Maybe now that we're a couple of weeks into this relationship, we need to go over the ground rules, make some changes. Can I come by after my meeting?"

Relief raced through her, stealing her breath, weakening her knees. She'd been afraid he was starting to let her down gently. Her heart stopped pounding against her chest like a bass drum in a parade. "Yes."

"How about we do something really different tonight?" he asked, a mischievous smile forming. "How about we just talk?"

She smiled back. "We can try."

He laughed, then they ran to their cars as rain pelted them. Between the soaking in the rain and the late hour, by the time she drove back to her house, she was starved. But not just for food.

She wanted something more. Much, much more. And she didn't think talking was going to satisfy that hunger.

Chapter Eleven

Rafe got home in time to change clothes and towel-dry his hair, Melina on his mind the whole time. Their relationship was about to undergo a change, one he wasn't sure either of them was prepared for. To spend time talking meant letting each other in. They'd both been hesitating about doing that. He knew fear drove him, but is that what drove her, too? That the past would catch up with them, and they'd have to deal with it instead of ignore it?

And would he get to stay overnight now, to sleep with her? It'd been a long time since he'd held her all night. The last time he'd done that they'd been committed to each other, with plans to marry and have children. Now they both seemed determined to avoid such commitments.

His doorbell rang. Ross was right on time. They pulled up a couple of bar stools at the kitchen counter, but before they opened the lid on the pepperoni pizza Ross had brought, he set the baggie holding the gold medallion on the counter next to Rafe. Then he added a second one.

Rafe looked them both over. "Duplicates?"

Ross nodded. "I knew it looked familiar. Bear with me here, because this is going to sound totally off the wall, but I woke up from a dream this morning, one in which Ryan Fortune appeared to me. Do you remember him?"

"Vaguely. He died a few years ago, right?"

"Of a brain tumor. His widow is Lily, who, as you know, was to marry William Fortune the day he disappeared."

"I'm following you so far."

"I know it had to be a dream, but I swear I saw Ryan's spirit at the foot of my bed, Rafe. He told me he hoped the medallion would help to reunite baby Anthony and his father—as if I knew who his father was. And that very second, I was sure where I'd seen that medallion. I had to hunt for it, but I finally found it with some family papers. My sister and brothers and I got these as Christmas gifts from our mother thirty-two years ago. I was ten years old."

"Are they more than trinkets, after all?" Rafe asked, intrigued.

"They're rare and expensive. At the time my mother told us a crazy story about their history that none of us believed, knowing her penchant for telling tales." He pushed up the lid of the pizza box. "I did what you suggested and had the medallion appraised. It's worth a small fortune. Because I had no choice, I called my mother, whom I rarely speak to, and asked where she got them, because I know she wouldn't have had enough money to buy them herself. After some prodding she told me that William Fortune had given them to her. Since he's gone missing, or possibly worse, I can't verify that story, but there's no reason not to believe her."

"So, your sister and brothers also have matching medallions?"

Ross nodded, then pulled a slice of pizza from the box. "I talked to my sister. She still has hers. I contacted my brother Flint, who's been living in upstate New York. He said he lost track of his medallion, but that he'd be on a plane down here within the next week. As for my brother Cooper, he's pretty much a nomad. When he checks in with one of us, we'll tell him what's going on. Who knows? Maybe Ryan Fortune's spirit will visit him and tell him to call home."

Rafe snagged a slice of pizza and let the story run through his head for a minute while he ate. "So, either Flint or Cooper must be the father? It's too much of a coincidence otherwise. Although it's odd that the baby was left without a note saying so."

"There's a lot that doesn't make sense. Yet. At least we can run DNA tests with Flint. Maybe Coop pawned his along the way—or something. But, as you say, it would be too coincidental for it to turn up in Red Rock around an abandoned baby's neck."

"To put it mildly. What does Jeremy say? Are he and Kirsten getting too attached to give up the baby when the time comes?"

"There's always that danger, but they seem committed to finding the parents. And you know, we keep talking about the father but forget we don't know the mother, either, now that Courtney has admitted she's not. What a mess." He looked bemused. "This is one of the most complicated cases I've ever worked on as a P.I., and it might turn out that the kid's my nephew."

The men finished up the pizza then Ross took off. Rafe decided to stop by Jeremy's place to see the baby for himself since he had time before heading to Melina's. Jeremy was performing a late, emergency surgery, Kirsten said, inviting him in. In the background, the baby cried.

"I'd given up walking him and put him in the swing, but that hasn't made him any happier. He's gotten a little spoiled because Jeremy walks him a lot." She looked askance at Rafe. "You wouldn't be interested in trying, would you? I fixed myself a bowl of soup, and it's getting cold."

For as much as he liked kids, Rafe hadn't held many babies, if any at all. Maybe a long time ago. "Go eat. Relax," he said, then walked to the swing and eyed the screaming infant. He lifted Anthony out then started walking and bouncing. His cries got louder. He had trouble catching his breath, he was crying so hard. So Rafe shifted him up to his shoulder and patted his back.

The crying slowed, bit by bit. Finally he drew a few shaky breaths, tucked his face against Rafe's neck and went to sleep. Rafe felt comforted himself, and happy that he'd been able to calm him.

Kirsten wandered in, a bowl in her hands, a smile on her face. "He must like men's voices better than women's. Thank you. Can you stay until Jeremy gets home from the hospital?" She laughed.

"Won't he sleep for a while?"

"If you hold him. If you put him down, all bets are off."

Rafe sat in a rocking chair, the baby's warm body against his, a living reminder of what he'd expected to have with Melina. Four kids *at least,* they'd decided. They would've had two by now, if all had gone to plan. He was surprised at the depth of emotions he felt thinking about it. It'd been off his radar for so long, he'd forgotten.

"You're a natural," Kirsten said, taking a seat on the sofa, pulling out baby clothes from a laundry basket to fold.

Eventually Jeremy returned. They talked for a little while about the medallion's connection to the Fortune family, then Rafe maneuvered the baby into Jeremy's arms, feeling an instant loss of warmth—and peace.

Rafe headed for Melina's, parking on the side street as usual. Maybe this wasn't the best time to have a talk with her. He hadn't realized how cheated he'd felt for all these years since their plan had gone awry.

Then again, maybe a little clearing of the air was just what the doctor ordered.

Melina was more edgy than on any of the other nights since Rafe had started coming over. Before, she'd been excited and anxious. Now her nerves felt close to the surface and prickly.

The plan was to talk. Would she learn things she didn't want to know? Would he? Would tonight move their relationship forward or push it back?

Maybe it would end it.

The idea made her breath catch. If they talked, if they were honest with each other, he might walk out and never come back.

That fear escalated when he knocked. She tried to steady herself, then went to the door, her knees shaking. He slipped inside her house quickly, as always, and shut the door.

He looked different. More serious. As apprehensive as she, his emotions just as close to the surface as hers.

She set her hands on his chest and looked him in the eye, something indefinable driving her to change their plans. "I think we should talk later."

He didn't even answer, but swept her into his arms

and headed up the stairs with her. With so much raw emotion between them, sex could either be mind blowing or devastating.

But life without risk wasn't life at all....

He laid her on her bed, followed her down and kissed her, not giving either of them time to come to their senses or change their minds. She felt no hesitance from him, no second thoughts, just need mixed with urgency. He was more aggressive and more driven, which was just fine with her. Soon, he let her take charge, her need just as powerful. She explored him. Cherished him. Welcomed him...

Couldn't get enough of him.

She tasted, taunted and teased, enjoying all the textures of his body, all the hitched breaths and sounds of arousal. How powerful that was, to bring about such a response.

She lingered, making the experience last, running her fingertips over him, following with her mouth, taking him almost to the brink several times, until he hauled her on top of him and helped her to lower herself onto him. She loved the sounds he made and the attention he paid to her body, so exposed to him. But he didn't last long after that. Nor did she. It was a wild ride of abandonment, tempered with fear and doubt and a tiny bit of hope. Nothing like it had happened before, not to this degree.

Would it ever happen again?

She ended up draped over him, his arms around her, their slick bodies adhering.

"Would you like to spend the night?" she asked, quietly, apprehensively.

Then came the answer she'd dreaded. "Before we go that far," he said. "Let's do what we intended to. Let's talk."

She rolled onto her side, facing him, dragging her fingertips along his neck, stalling.

"You smell like baby powder," she said.

"I just came from visiting Jeremy and Kirsten." He put a hand on hers, stopping her exploration. "The baby needed calming. For some reason, he took to me."

"Just like Elliot."

"Melina." His expression was so serious. "Why are you evading?"

Because I'm scared. "I don't know."

He got out of bed, grabbed her hand and pulled her up. When they were dressed, they settled in on her couch downstairs. She sat at the opposite end, facing him, her knees up.

"On the subject of Elliot's attachment to you," she said, finding a safe place to start. "I called Q when I got home, then I spoke with Elliot's parents. Elliot knows about Asperger's in theory, but he doesn't really understand the complexities of it, so his parents work with him issue by issue as they come up. Baseball is a big-picture issue—physical, mental and emotional elements come into play."

"So, nothing can be done about his strong connection to me? It's too complicated to try?"

"They'll talk to him about how it looks to the other kids when he's not fully involved in the game, so that would be your cue. Remind him what his goal is. It should work. If not, we'll try something else. It's important that he doesn't obsess about you, because it's very hard to break an obsession, which you've probably guessed from how he's always quoting your stats."

"His parents sure have a lot to deal with."

"Parents are the unsung heroes of the world, for so many reasons."

"Even temporary ones, like Kirsten and Jeremy taking care of a baby they have no ties to."

"Your mom would've done that," Melina said. She rested her chin on her upraised knees, looking at him directly, wondering once more where this conversation—this long-overdue conversation—would take them, while still aching pleasantly from their lovemaking. "She seemed happiest when she was taking care of everyone."

"As do you."

His tone sounded matter-of-fact, and yet his body language was at odds with that, not nearly as relaxed. "I'm not totally selfless," she said.

"People like to talk about you to me," he said, his eyes smiling at the absurdity of it all. "You are the champion do-gooder of Red Rock."

"Is that a compliment or a criticism?"

"I guess it's somewhere in the middle." He held up

a hand. "I know. I have no right to make those kinds of comments."

She thought that over for a few seconds. "It seems to me that this *is* the time for that, now that our initial sexual attraction has settled down."

His brows went up. "Settled down? That's what you call—" he pointed toward the ceiling "—that?"

"You know what I mean."

"I don't think I do. I want you as much now as I did our first time. Probably even more than then. It's far from settled down for me. And I haven't detected any lessening of desire from you. Just the opposite, in fact."

"Wow. Okay. This really is going to be a serious discussion," she said, even more worried about the outcome. "Yes, I want you even more than ever. But, there are walls between us, Rafe."

He nodded. "I'm looking to start the next stage of my life, Melina. I didn't know that when I made the decision to come home. I thought it was to help my dad, and certainly that was number one in my reasoning, but I'm making a new life here. A complete life. I hadn't realized how shallow my existence had been these past few years. As I told you, I'd had one goal in mind—success. I liked the money and prestige. I have a knack for buying and selling, and I don't even know where it came from. It's just instinct."

"How'd you manage to take the time to help Elliot?"

"I made time. Put off some other things."

"*Why* did you?" she asked, since it didn't seem to fit with running a successful law practice.

He was quiet awhile, then, "Because you asked. I haven't done anything I haven't been paid to do for a long time. Maybe never. I don't remember."

"It's incredibly rewarding. Helping people," she added. "If I hadn't taken care of my grandmother for that year, I never would've known about this field of work—or how good I would be at it."

"Tell me about that."

Showtime, she thought. The beginning of what had become the end of their relationship. "You were with me when I got the news about her stroke. We'd been at Ann Arbor for, what, three months? Mom and Dad talked me out of coming home until Christmas break."

"Then you never went back to college."

"I couldn't. You saw that. Gramps wasn't in the best of health, so he couldn't assume the load. My mom worked full-time. Angie and Stephanie were too young." She leaned across the space between her and Rafe and touched his arm. "I missed *you,* but I found I really didn't miss college."

"I loved every minute of it."

"I know. I did, too, once I found my calling and started studying in the right field. Not that caring for Grandma Rose was easy. It wasn't. It was really, really hard, physically and emotionally. Plus Gramps was difficult to deal with. He was so afraid he would lose her. A year later, when she did die, he went into such deep mourning we thought he'd never come out of it. As I'm sure you've heard, I stayed on at his house for a year more."

"He seems to be okay now."

"He put up quite a fuss when I told him I was moving out, but it was past time. Mom and Dad have offered to have him live with them, and I imagine he'll do that at some point. I'm not sure how well Mom will make that transition." Melina smiled at the idea. Her father was hard enough to live with. "It was good of you to invite your father to live with you."

"It's hard to see your parent become scared, or worse, dependent." He laid his hand on her feet and squeezed. "I guess I finally understand what drove you to take such a drastic step, to quit college to care for your grandma."

"Do you? I don't think I even really understood then. I just knew someone had to help, and I seemed to be the only one available. It wasn't until a couple of weeks ago, after you got back, and I started reflecting on it all, that I realized once and for all that I wasn't cut out to be a lawyer. I wouldn't have been any good at it. I rationalized my leaving school because of my grandparents, when it was just as much my own desire." Her eyes stung at the admission. "See? I'm selfish, after all."

She took a breath, then said what she'd been needing to say for years. "Being away from you was hard enough while I was helping them 24/7, but having you break up with me at the same time just about did me in."

He let go of her feet. His jaw went hard. "A lot of people have alluded to the fact I broke up with you. Melina. I've kept quiet about it because I wasn't the one living here, and I understood you wanted to keep people's good opinion of you. But since we both know that's not how it happened, maybe it's time you at least acknowledge that for me, if no one else."

His anger was palpable. She felt the heat of it travel to her, adding to her own. "What do you mean, you didn't break up with me?"

"You think I did?"

What a ridiculous question. "Of course I do. I even have proof."

He sat up straight. "Okay."

"Okay, what?"

"Prove it."

"You don't know? Seriously?"

"If I knew, I wouldn't ask. You say you have proof. I want to see it."

She pushed herself up, her muscles bunched and taut. "I'll be happy to," she said, then she ran upstairs as her heart pounded.

The time had come.

Chapter Twelve

Rafe got up, as well, then didn't know what to do with himself, so he went into her kitchen and poured a glass of water, standing at the sink to drink it.

This hadn't been what he'd had in mind when he'd suggested they just talk tonight. He'd wanted to know about the past ten years. He'd wanted to know about her work. He hadn't wanted to dig into the painful ending of their relationship....

Except it had to come out sometime, and the no-strings-affair wasn't working. It wasn't enough. So, it was time to clear the air—even if it muddied the waters.

She came down the stairs and directly into the kitchen, handing him a picture frame. But instead of a photograph inside it, there was a typed note, a letter from him to her.

Melina, I don't know any other way to get through to you. I've been patient long enough. You've made decisions without taking me into consideration, and that says it all to me. So, I give up. I'm done. You made your choice. Good luck with that. Rafe

He remembered every detail of the note now that he'd seen it again, reliving every emotion. Anger and betrayal surged through him anew as he realized what he held. "You framed it? You framed my note?"

She crossed her arms. "Darn right I did."

His jaw hurt, sending shards of pain down his body. "I see I was wrong. Your silence back then didn't say it all. *This* did." He handed it back to her, then walked toward her door, not looking back.

Suddenly she was there, behind him. "Oh, sure. Walk out. At least this time it's in person, not by letter."

He spun around, trying to rein in his temper. She'd framed his note. Of all the— "That letter was a damned sight more effort than you ever put in. The least you could have done was return my calls. Even just one call."

Her brows drew together. "What? When?"

"Oh, come on, Melina. Be honest, at least. I called for weeks."

"Only a couple of times."

Fury teemed in him. No one ever questioned his integrity. "Many times. Why would I lie to you? You didn't own a cell phone then, but I left messages. I talked with your grandfather. *You* never called me back. Not to tell me what was going on, or how your grandmother was doing, or even when you were coming back to school. Nothing."

She shook her head. "My grandfather would have told me. I only remember two calls."

"I *called*. A lot. Then when I gave up and sent you the letter, all you did was send me back the promise ring in the mail, with a note that just said *okay,* I might add."

She crossed her arms. "I was too hurt."

"You think I wasn't? I went through hell."

They stared at each other, tension crackling between them.

"I guess it shows how wrong we were for each other," she said, voicing aloud what he'd just figured out. "It would've ended at some point. Maybe not that soon or painfully, but sometime."

"Unlike you, I never saw my future without you in it," he said honestly. "You were all I wanted."

"You think I didn't feel the same? I applied to Michigan because of you. I didn't want to leave home, but, even more, I didn't want to leave you."

His gut clenched. "Why is this the first I'm hearing about that? Why didn't you tell me?"

She threw up her hands. "I was young and in love. You convinced me that it would be an adventure, and it was, but not in a good way for me. And, honestly, I would've made a lousy lawyer."

"So you grasped at the first opportunity to come back home instead of telling me, and letting us deal with it together?"

"I was eighteen years old! I'd been sheltered all my life, Rafe. I got scared. You were enjoying yourself, and I wasn't. I could see myself getting clingier all the time. You even made a comment about it."

Rafe thought back, recalling a vague memory that she'd become more and more dependent on him. "I didn't know it was that serious."

"I didn't know, either. I couldn't make sense of it. I just knew I was worried all the time. So, yes, I guess I did use my grandmother as an opportunity to come home again. But I loved you, and missed you."

I loved you. Past tense. He didn't know why it hurt so much to hear it put like that. "So you're saying you were too immature?"

"Without a doubt. Not that I acknowledged it then, but I've done so much soul searching since you came back. In retrospect, a lot has come clear to me. All these things I've just told you are new to me, too. I don't think I wanted to look back, and having you here forced me to."

He saw desperation in her eyes, as if willing him to understand. As if begging to be held, too, but he was careful not to touch her, not knowing how he felt now. He looked at the framed letter again, and the stab of pain returned in full force. She'd kept the damn letter—*framed*. Who did that?

"I need time to sort this out," he said and saw her

retreat, not physically, but emotionally. "I know we'll see each other because of Elliot."

"Whatever." She turned away.

He had to go. Had to get away from…everything. He didn't even say goodbye, but left. Outside the cool air felt good against his skin. Too restless to go home, Rafe drove to Red, hoping to catch his brother, not knowing his schedule for the week.

When there was no one up front to greet him, Rafe took a seat at the bar.

Wendy Fortune moseyed over. "It's a slow night. Marcos is running the bar as well as managing. He's in the kitchen, but he'll be out in a sec. Do you want something to eat?"

Did he? Even a drink didn't sound good, but he probably could use both. "How about a half order of nachos with chicken, please?"

"Sure thing." She grinned at Marcos over her shoulder as he reached the bar, then she headed for the kitchen, her hips twitching a little more evidently.

"When are you going to admit you've got a thing for her?" Rafe asked his brother as he pulled a cold draft.

"The day you admit you've still got a thing for Melina."

Rafe hesitated, then said, "Well, then you'd better start figuring out where to take Wendy on your first date."

Marcos said nothing, but his mouth tightened. He waited as Rafe took a long sip.

Rafe finally set down the glass. "Remember when you said I should give you something harder to figure out?" he asked his brother.

Marcos leaned both arms against the bar. "I do."

"Women, Marcos. I don't understand women."

"What's going on?"

"I don't want to talk about it. I just want words of wisdom. Go ahead, speak in generalities."

"Can't live with 'em. Can't live without sex. One of 'em has to give."

"You're not helpful."

"Give me specifics."

Wendy came up with his order of nachos. "Woman trouble, Rafe?" she asked, her eyes full of sympathy.

Rafe stared back.

She patted his hand. "You men have perfected the look. Hangdog, you know?"

Hangdog? Him? That made him straighten up. She patted his hand again, turned a sparkly gaze on Marcos for a minute then strode off, humming to the classical guitar music always playing in the background.

"Don't start," Marcos said. "Wendy and I had an argument right before you came in. She's impervious to criticism. She says no one has given her less than a twenty-percent tip, so she must be doing her job well."

"If no one's complained, why do you care?"

Marcos stared off in the direction she'd gone.

"Beats me. Something about her drives me crazy. But let's get back to you."

Rafe realized he needed to think things through for himself, not get feedback in generalities. He'd learned more about Melina in a couple of hours tonight than in the weeks they'd been seeing each other.

After a while he went home. Tonight they'd each revealed the truth as they'd seen it. Who was right? Both? Neither?

Did it even matter any more?

How did someone recover? Maybe it wasn't possible.

And maybe it was just time to accept that and move on.

Melina didn't sleep after he left, not well, anyway, or deeply. When her phone rang the next morning, she knew it would be him.

"I didn't sleep much," he said.

"Me, either."

A few unbearable seconds of silence followed, then, "I need to step away," he said, breaking her heart. "I want to move forward, Melina. A sex-only relationship with you isn't going to make that happen."

"I understand," she said, not really understanding. But it was her turn to give him space. Maybe it would turn out differently from when *she'd* needed space all those years ago. "I'll see you at the ballpark."

He didn't say anything, so she said, "Goodbye, Rafe," her throat aching and eyes burning.

"Bye."

"I love you," she whispered after she'd hung up. "I'll always love you." He was her mate, had always been her mate. It had taken time to see that, and some pain, too, but she couldn't deny the truth any longer. She loved him as a woman, not a girl. Forever. She wanted more than just sex, too.

She wouldn't settle for less.

Now she had to figure out how to win him back.

Chapter Thirteen

When Melina arrived at her grandfather's house later that morning, he told her he was driving his truck, and she couldn't argue. He'd rigged a step device that let him to climb into the vehicle, then he could pull it into the cab and stow it in the backseat.

Melina settled into the passenger seat, Rafe still on her mind.

"What's got your ears floppin', missy?" her grandfather asked as he started the engine.

"I'm okay."

"Nope. I've seen the signs before. I'd say it's man trouble."

The way he said it, dragging out the word "man," made her laugh. "Maybe it's lack-of-man trouble," she said. "As in, being twenty-nine years old and not having a man."

"Maybe. Doubt it, but maybe." He navigated his driveway and started up the street. His truck was an automatic, so he didn't have to use a clutch. Melina wasn't sure he could have.

"Been a while since I drove ol' Trigger," he said. "I forgot how heavy-handed he is."

"You're the only man I know who doesn't refer to his vehicle as a she."

"Some vehicles are *shes*. Some aren't. This one's reliable and powerful. Can't be female."

Melina laughed again, the knots in her stomach loosening. "Do you feel ready for your driving test?"

"Don't have much choice, do I? It's two days off. Now or never. And I sure don't want somebody having to take me grocery shopping or whatever forever. Wouldn't feel like much of a man then, that's for sure."

"We all wish you'd take Mom and Dad up on their offer to have you live with them."

"Everyone except your mom and dad." He gave her a sly glance. "Oh, sure, they offered. What decent son and daughter-in-law wouldn't? But they've only had an empty nest for a year. They're still on their second honeymoon."

Melina hadn't thought of it like that. "You're very wise."

"Supposed to be by now. Your grandma accused

me of arrested development for a long time, but I think I finally grew up."

He reached the downtown, where traffic was a little more congested and he had to make decisions rather than just drive. He was doing better than when he drove her car. Maybe it was the familiarity.

"Want to head to San Antonio?" she asked. "You should probably get some freeway time in."

"I know my limitations. I'll drive in Red Rock but no farther. No sense tempting fate."

She wondered what had gotten into him. He was much more mellow today, was even seeing his future clearly. Maybe driving his truck again had been enough to restore his confidence.

He pulled into the grocery store parking lot. "I need a few things. Okay with you?"

"You can use your hour however you want to, Gramps."

He aimed for a space close to the front of the store, then shut off the engine. Before she opened her door, she said, "Did Rafe come to see you?"

"No. Why would he?"

After a minute she shrugged. She'd hoped Rafe had come to the same conclusions she had during the night, especially once she'd calmed down enough to realize that he wouldn't lie to her. If he said he'd called, he had.

"Something you want to talk about, missy?"

Her heart started to pound hard, but she had to

know. "When I was living with you and Grandma, did Rafe call me? Did he leave messages?"

"'Course he did. I told you."

"More than twice?" she asked, although she didn't think his answer would surprise her much.

He stared out the windshield. "Maybe a few more. But you specifically told me you didn't want to talk to him."

"Not forever. I just needed some time to adjust." She'd known that Rafe would try to talk her out of staying. She hadn't wanted to argue with him. She'd had enough on her plate.

"How was I supposed to know that?" Gramps asked.

She looked him in the eye, saying nothing, accusing him but also acknowledging her own part in what had happened.

"Okay," he said. "I didn't want you to leave us. I couldn't help Rose on my own. I figured you'd hightail it back to school—and Rafe—as soon as you could. I know it was wrong."

"You think?" She thought of the framed letter, and humiliation washed over her. She'd been such a fool. She hadn't trusted him. How differently things would've turned out if she'd talked to him.

And yet, maybe not. He was right that she'd never called him, but had selfishly waited for him to do the calling—and then had thought he hadn't bothered. Maybe talking wouldn't have made any difference at all. She hadn't wanted to face the truth—that she didn't want to go back to college.

They'd both been so young and foolish, with no life experience yet, no romantic experience except with each other.

"Are you and Rafe fighting because of what I did?" Gramps asked. "I'll go to him. Talk to him."

"No." She tempered the harsh word with, "Please don't. Promise you won't. This is between Rafe and me. Period." What her grandfather had done was part of the problem but not all of it.

He look relieved. "I can promise you that."

He spent the rest of his hour making nice to her, even being cooperative about following her directions to take a different route home, seeing if he could do it without getting lost. He did fine.

When they reached his house, everything was okay between them again.

"You're a good girl. Thank you for helping me," he said.

"My pleasure, Gramps." She kissed him goodbye and went on to see Big John, hoping he was in as mellow a mood as her grandfather. She really didn't feel like coaxing him today. She had too much on her mind. For example, now that she knew the truth about what had kept her and Rafe apart, what difference did it make? She'd already come to realize that they were both vastly different people now. Maybe they would've been like June and Wade, getting a divorce, having outgrown each other.

Time would tell.

Later that afternoon Rafe met Debbie Anderson in the sports complex parking lot as usual. Elliot hopped out of her car.

"Hi, Rafe Mendoza!" he shouted as he ran around the rear of the car.

"Please tell Melina we talked to him," Debbie said. "Keep reinforcing the fact he needs to remember he's on a team and they're counting on him, okay?"

"Got it. Hey, sport," Rafe said to Elliot, who smiled more spontaneously than Rafe had ever seen. "All set?"

"Ready, set, go!"

"Bye, sweetie," Debbie called out.

"Bye. Let's go, Rafe Mendoza."

"Here comes Melina. We always wait for each other, remember?" Rafe didn't know what he could say to her. The fact she hadn't believed that he'd called her so many times weighed heavy. He'd thought they had a relationship based on trust. Everything he'd been learning lately indicated there was no truth to that. She'd never told him how she felt, how much she'd hated college. He didn't understand why she didn't feel she could tell him.

The problem was—he still wanted her. His need hadn't diminished since he was fourteen years old. He should have gotten past that by now. He could control everything else in his life except his desire for her.

It's one of those relationships that's only physical, he decided. No more, no less. And physical could be conquered, although probably only by not being around her. Which was impossible, given their connection through Elliot.

"Hi, guys," Melina said, a little too brightly, as she jogged up to them, her gaze on Elliot.

"Let's play," Elliot said. "Can I go to the field myself?"

Because he would be in their line of sight the whole time, there was no reason not to let him run, to be like the other boys—except it would leave Rafe and Melina alone. "Sure," Rafe said, not willing to deny Elliot's request. "We'll catch up."

Elliot took off running, not a smooth lope but a determined one. He'd already matured just in a few weeks.

Rafe and Melina walked silently side by side. He had nothing to say.

After a minute Melina said, "If you want to go ahead, feel free."

"Thanks." Relieved, he took off running. They had only two more team practices before opening day. He needed to focus on Elliot now. Only Elliot.

"Trouble in paradise?" Beau asked as Rafe reached home plate, where Beau stood, watching the boys warm up but obviously aware of tension between Rafe and Melina.

Rafe ignored him, peripherally aware of her settling in the dugout, where she pulled her cap low and tossed a ball into her glove, again and again and again, her usual activity during practice, even though she'd created a solid pocket in her glove by now.

"We need to talk about the boy," Beau said, bringing Rafe to attention.

"What about him?"

"It doesn't look to me like he'll be ready next week."

Rafe watched Elliot doing stretches with the rest of the team, his expression serious. Single-minded. "He'll be ready. And you need his bat. He's the best hitter you've got."

"He also has to play defense for at least a couple of innings every game."

"He's working hard, Beau. Give him a shot."

"I need to win. You know that."

"You need to have a heart, too. Just playing is a win for Elliot."

Beau crossed his arms. He looked at the boys, not Rafe. "The other kids haven't taken to him."

"I know. Relating is a tough skill for him. But I've seen some changes, and expect there will be more."

"We'll see."

Rafe started to walk away when Beau said, "It really was an accident, me hitting him. Because of my injury. I didn't want to admit it was hindering my game, even at this level."

Rafe wasn't feeling sympathetic at this point. "Yeah? Well, don't use a kid as your scapegoat again." He leaned close, tired of his life spinning out of control, needing to take action, to do something. "If you deny Elliot the right to play, you can expect to see us in court. I'll file a civil suit so fast your head will spin. Wouldn't be good PR, either, no matter how it ended."

Rafe didn't feel any better for having chewed out Beau. Maintaining his cool was something that Rafe had gotten good at. Really good at. For all his good intentions, he wasn't moving forward, wasn't finding peace. It had all been made worse overnight, it seemed.

And there she sat in the dugout, a visible reminder of the havoc one woman could wreak on a man's life.

He needed to do something about that.

Melina barely watched the practice. She jabbed at the dirt floor with the toes of her sneakers, kicking up dust.

"Someone's not happy." June took a seat beside Melina, eyeing her thoughtfully.

The last thing Melina wanted was for the town crier to have more gossip to spread. "Just restless. I wish I could be out on the field."

June's brows went up.

"I know," Melina said with a sigh. "In high school I was the world's biggest klutz. I've been helping Rafe work with Elliot. Sometimes I can even catch a fly ball." She smiled at the memory of her one catch, which had taken everyone by surprise—all of her family and Rafe's, who'd been recruited to help act as a team.

"That *would* be newsworthy," June said, grinning.

"Ha-ha. So, are you still working on the story about Beau?"

"Yes. I've been able to take my time because the editor isn't running it until the season opens next week. He decided to put out a special issue just about Red Rock baseball. I've got most of the bylines."

"Good for you, June."

"You know what I've learned? There are four kids known to have Asperger's playing on various teams."

Melina did know that. Two of them were Q's patients, but since they didn't have Beau as a coach, they didn't have as much to prove, plus they'd all played ball before. Just as important, they'd been living in town when registration closed, which seemed to be key to Beau.

"I'd like to do a story about it, but I've run up against total resistance from all the parents. Which I understand," June added quickly. "The kids don't want to be seen as different. But I was thinking maybe I could do a story on you, and incorporate information about autism and Asperger's."

"My partner is the one to talk to. It's his specialty. I work mostly with stroke and accident victims—and also the elderly who want to continue to live alone. *That* would be a good story, I think. Timely. There's a huge, aging population trying to figure out how to stay independent."

"Let me run it by my editor. Sounds good to me."

They sat side by side without talking for a while.

"So, Rafe got ticked at me for doing a little online speculation that you two were back together," June said, "but you haven't said anything."

Her sister Stephanie had been the first to point out the item to Melina, but not the last. She hadn't taken the bait. "We're not back together." Melina could say that honestly now. "Elliot's a team endeavor, that's all."

"Yeah, I heard that Rafe didn't leave town this week, as usual. I wondered if that would hurt his business."

Leave town? Melina didn't want to seem ignorant, but she had no idea what June meant. "It's nice to be your own boss."

"But it doesn't really matter, does it? You're still always working for someone."

Melina couldn't disagree with her.

June fidgeted. "So, the reason I asked about Rafe is that I didn't want to step on any toes. I'll be honest, Melina. He interests me."

Dread filled Melina's body from top to toe. She

felt frozen in place. "I thought you were interested in Beau."

"He's pretty messed up. Rafe's got his head on straight. And he likes kids, which is important, since I've got two."

Melina hesitated, then said, "You know, I've heard from a whole lot of people that you should take a little time for yourself when a relationship ends. Time to heal."

"I'm not looking for serious. Just someone to hang out with."

Well, Rafe's looking for serious, Melina thought. He's ready to get married and start a family. So it wasn't really fair of June to—

She stopped the thought cold. Rafe was a big boy. He could take care of himself, make up his mind just fine on his own.

She searched the field for him, spotted him hunkered down in front of Elliot, talking to him, Elliot nodding back. Maybe Rafe *had* agreed to help because of her, as he'd said, but he was fully invested in the outcome now, and their common cause would keep them tied together for the two months of baseball season, so there was no hope of breaking all contact.

I want him. Need him. Love him. The words hammered her brain. She couldn't bear for June—or anyone else—to have him. She couldn't give up. Now that she knew the truth about what had kept them apart, now that they'd both grown up and knew their own minds better, it could be so different for them. Not sex only, but the whole deal.

She watched him running beside Elliot, encouraging him. What a wonderful father he would make—

What if she took a different tack altogether? What if instead of trying to avoid him, she put herself squarely in front of him at every opportunity? What if she acted as if nothing had happened between them? What if she became superfriend? Dazzle him with confusion.

She felt laughter bubble inside her. She wouldn't mind seeing him confused by an all-out assault of happiness.

She took a quick look at June, who had suddenly become the competition. Melina was up for a little competition, needed some, actually. Her life had become static, going nowhere. She went to work each day, then met Rafe secretly at night. What had that resulted in? Great sex? Sure. What else?

Not much. But they hadn't given it a chance, either, beyond her bedroom.

So before she gave up altogether, she needed to give it one last shot—on her own terms.

With a little luck, he would never know what hit him. She'd given up on him before. He deserved to know she didn't want to give up now. He could make up his mind from there.

She laughed then, feeling good, feeling free of

all the pressures of the past weeks. She'd already survived losing him once. She could do it again, if she had to.

But this time she planned to win.

Chapter Fourteen

Five days later, Melina and her mother were slicing tomatoes and onions for the hamburgers that her father was grilling on the patio. It was Elliot's last day of training in her family's backyard, and they were feeding thirteen people—everyone who'd been helping form a practice team.

However, this day was different from the rest. It was all for fun. Melina knew that Rafe's goal was to get Elliot to loosen up, to laugh, deciding that would help him more in the long run.

Melina hoped so. Tomorrow would be the final team practice, when Beau would make his decision, and the next day, his first game, if he passed muster.

"You look happy," Patsy Lawrence said to her daughter.

"I am happy, Mom," Melina answered. She'd barely stopped smiling for days. Rafe was utterly confused. Melina loved it. "Elliot's in the home stretch, Gramps passed his driver's test, Q and I both have full caseloads. Life's good."

"You didn't mention Rafe." Patsy pulled a head of lettuce apart and rinsed the leaves. "Is he part of your happiness quotient?"

"He's the unknown-X factor."

Patsy eyed her. "That's the first time you haven't denied there was something between you."

"Because hope triumphs over reality."

Her mother seemed to let that sink in. "So, you want something to happen, but it's not happening?"

"Yet."

Patsy laid a hand on Melina's arm. "Haven't you been hurt enough?"

"Things are different this time, Mom." She had already decided not to tell her parents what Gramps had done. That was then, and this is now. "There's really no one else for me but Rafe."

"Of course there is, honey. There are a lot of people in this big world we can love."

"Rafe's my mate. For life."

"Does he know that? Does he feel the same?"

"Deep inside, yes." She just had to mine down that far. Drill past the barriers. "But don't worry. I'm not being patient. I'm going for it. It's now or never."

She would've made more progress by now, too, except that he'd left town for the weekend. She'd had a moment's ridiculous worry that he'd gone away with June, then she'd seen June at the grocery store. Melina hadn't really believed he would jump into a situation like that right away, anyway, but sometimes the heart asked questions instead of the head. The point was, she was determined not to live with regrets for not trying.

"You're *chasing* him?" Patsy asked, sounding appalled.

"I seem to remember a story you told me once about how you had to chase Dad to catch him. And don't you dare say that was different. The approach may be different, and the particular circumstances, but the goal is the same. I want to marry him. I want children with him." Every time she drove by the old Crockett building they'd decided years ago to buy, she wanted a life with him even more. It was a small building but it loomed large to her for what it represented.

And at Angie's wedding reception, he'd wondered why it hadn't been demolished by now.

Maybe ten years had passed, and maybe they'd both changed, sought different career paths, but they were at their cores the same people with the same values. They both worked hard, cared about others, wanted a family of their own. Even if old buildings didn't mean the same thing to both of them.

Melina heard her mother sigh.

"What can I do to help?" Patsy asked.

Smiling, Melina hugged her. "Try to keep Dad calm when I openly flirt with Rafe."

"Oh, sure. Give me the easy job."

Melina laughed.

"Ready out here!" her father called from the porch. "You ready in there?"

"Tell everyone to come wash up!" Patsy called back.

As people cleaned up and were walking back outside, they were given something to carry. Two picnic tables and a few extra chairs were enough to hold everyone—all of Melina's family, Rafe's and Elliot's. Elliot's mother had made cupcakes decorated to look like baseballs. Lemonade flowed, as did conversation and laughter.

Melina carried her plate to where Rafe sat with his brothers and father and took the empty seat next to him, bumping shoulders as she settled in.

"Mind if I sit here?" she asked Rafe, after the fact, smiling at his family then at him.

He subtly maneuvered his body away from hers enough not to touch. "Make yourself at home."

The dry way he said it made her laugh. When she made eye contact with Marcos, he grinned, too.

"Food's good," she said, digging into her potato salad.

"I haven't been to a family barbecue in a long time," Marcos said. "As good as the food at Red tastes, nothing beats a homemade burger. So, how was the trip to Ann Arbor?" he asked Rafe.

"Productive."

He'd gone to Michigan? Was that what June had been talking about? Did he take a "usual trip" to Ann Arbor? Was there a woman—

"I'm closing up my office there," he added. "I can fly up occasionally, if necessary, but there's little I can't do by phone and email. Teleconferencing is easy these days, even with video. Saves us all time and money."

Melina let the conversation drift around her, piecing together the facts. Apparently, before he'd moved home, he'd promised three companies in Ann Arbor he would spend a week every month in town. It was easy to figure out that he hadn't gone north for a week this month because of his commitment to Elliot, one that would continue for two more months.

He hadn't said a word about it, hadn't even hinted at it. He'd accepted Beau's rules, knowing he wouldn't be able to meet his other obligations, the ones that paid him.

After dinner, Rafe's brother Javier played guitar and sang, joined by Melina's grandfather. They sang old cowboy songs, bringing back childhood memories for Melina, who still sat next to Rafe.

"There's room over here with us," her father said, patting an empty spot on the bench next to him.

"I'm good, thanks," Melina said. Her mother whispered in his ear. He frowned, looked at Melina then

Rafe and frowned a little more, but he didn't repeat the offer the rest of the night.

Rafe's back was to her as they listened to the music. She ached to lean against him, to slip her arms around him. Instead she just leaned close enough that her breath would dust his neck when she spoke. "They're really good together, Gramps and Javier. Who would've guessed it?"

He looked over his shoulder. "Good thing you and I aren't singing."

She laughed. Neither of them could carry a tune.

It seemed like an easy summer evening, yet it was late March and a school night for Elliot. His parents took him home under protest, then the others started drifting away, too. Kitchen cleanup went fast. Melina expected Rafe to have left by the time she was done with the dishes, but he still sat in the backyard with his father.

"I'd forgotten how nice these family events are," his father said. "Elena always planned our parties. I miss them."

"I'll get a barbecue up and running soon, Dad," Rafe said.

"Thank you. You are a good son, Rafe. A good man."

A moment of silence followed as Rafe reached for his father's hand and squeezed. Melina felt like an intruder into their private moment, but then his father stood.

"Well, this old man needs his sleep. Good night." He made his way across the yard to the driveway and disappeared.

Rafe and Melina were alone. She wondered why her father wasn't hovering, then decided her mother was probably making him stay inside.

"This was nice," he said.

"Yes."

"You seem to be doing okay, Melina."

She smiled. "I am." She decided not to ask if he was okay, too, but to let him tell her what he wanted to. She'd found a storehouse of patience within her determination to have him again. "So, tomorrow we find out if Beau will allow Elliot to play," she said. She rested her arm on the table, her hand an inch from his. She could almost feel him. Almost.

"I'm not worried about it," he said, looking at their hands then back at her.

"Do you think Beau's going to let him play?" she asked.

"I do."

"I know Elliot's come a long way, but he still has a lot of trouble in the field." She felt Rafe's fingertips brush hers—or had they? It might have been wishful thinking on her part. "His catching has improved, but he can't throw the ball in far or straight."

"He needs more practice, that's all." He moved back a little. "June came to see me."

Her hopeful mood made a U-turn. "Oh?"

"She wanted me to represent her in her divorce."

"Oh, really?" Melina couldn't keep the sarcasm out of her voice. So *that* was how June was playing it? Everyone knew Rafe didn't do family law. "Are you going to?"

"No. Not my specialty, although that hasn't stopped some other people from seeking me out lately. Like you."

Melina couldn't get a handle on him. Was he trying to entice her with elusive touches, or was that a diversion while he talked to her about another woman?

"Technically, *Angie* did that," Melina said, starting to cross her arms, then remembering her goal was to win him back. "I never would have."

"Things have a way of working out. It was an interesting conversation with June, however. Apparently she has your blessing to ask me out."

Well, how…blatant of the woman. "All I did was tell her no, that we weren't together."

"Do you think I'd be interested in a woman newly separated from her husband, Melina? A man I consider a friend, by the way."

"Did you hear what I just said? I only answered her question. No, we aren't together." She made herself seem unperturbed by the conversation. She even smiled. "I think you and I have both learned the hard way that honesty's the best policy, and all that."

"Plus, you knew I wouldn't be interested in June."

Which wasn't entirely true. "No, I didn't. I don't

know what kind of woman you go for these days. Other than for sex, that is."

She waited for several long seconds for him to respond, but all he did was stand. "I should get going."

She walked with him, grabbing her purse from the back stairs where she'd left it. Her car was in the driveway. His was at the curb. They stopped next to her driver's door.

"You're up to something," he said.

"I am?" Her smile widened.

"The Cheshire-cat grin doesn't fool me. I know you too well."

If he knew her that well, he would know she'd fallen in love with him again. He would know that her heart and future were in his hands. "I'm just being myself."

He stared into her eyes, murmured good-night, then walked away, hardly making a sound.

She felt instantly lonely.

And just a little bit more hopeful than she had this morning.

Rafe hurled his mitt into his trunk, slammed the lid shut then climbed into his car, all the while watching Melina back out of the driveway then take off down the road. He could almost hear her whistling happily as she went.

He'd had a hell of a week.

First had been his decision to step back from

Melina, then his threat to take Beau to court if he didn't leave Elliot on the team. Then June had put the moves on him, leaving him in the awkward position of turning her down when she was most vulnerable. And then he'd had to ask for a weekend meeting with his Michigan clients to tell them he wouldn't be as available as he'd been. To top it all off, his flight home had been delayed for six hours, so he'd barely had any sleep last night.

And now Melina was changing right before his eyes. She was way too...happy. Like the Melina he used to know, not the one he'd met since he came back. Apparently, ending their relationship was a good thing for her.

He wanted her more than ever.

Rafe had to drive by her house on the way to his. He could see her taillights ahead of him and slowed to a crawl as she parked and walked toward her court-yard, turning at the last minute, staring in his direction, lifting a hand in a tentative wave.

He took off, angry at himself. What would she think? That he was stalking her?

He was too tired. Too confused. Too much in de-mand. He needed to slow his pace, his goal when he'd first come home. He needed to make some life decisions, too.

Rafe headed for his shower as soon as he got home. He stood under the spray, his hands pressed to the wall, water pounding his neck and shoulders... missing her.

He'd been missing the Melina he'd seen tonight, the bright, infectious woman he'd fallen in love with. That Melina hadn't made many appearances the past few weeks. Sexy, yes. Dedicated, yes. But the woman who'd loved life and lived it so joyously had been AWOL since…

Since Ann Arbor, ten years ago.

He had noticed she wasn't happy when they'd started college, but he'd chalked it up to being homesick, to the pressures of college courses. He hadn't looked deeper than that because he hadn't wanted to. He'd been having fun. His world had expanded in immeasurable ways. Hers had narrowed.

He hadn't paid attention.

Tonight she'd been the girl who'd graduated from high school with him, fun and flirtatious, but now also independent. That was what was different. She'd been dependent on him at college, for companionship, for studying together, for social connections—totally unlike the Melina of high school.

And now? Now she was like that Melina, but more. So much more. Since they'd started their secret relationship he hadn't been looking at the big picture, but pieces of it. Sex had blurred the lines too much.

Rafe turned off the shower, dried off, then dragged himself to bed, the lost sleep from the previous night catching up.

But as he lay in bed he realized something critical had happened tonight—his doubts about the future had dimmed. He'd needed forward momentum, something to drive him, instead of just spinning his wheels.

He'd needed to break up with Melina in order to start over.

He'd done that. Now he only needed a new plan.

It was as simple—and complicated—as that.

Chapter Fifteen

Melina arrived at the final practice the next day earlier than usual, intent on advancing her plan to change Rafe's mind. She sat in her car, watching the parking lot entrance, waiting for him to arrive, optimistic about seeing him again.

He didn't show. Nor did Elliot.

Worried, she called Rafe's phone but only got his voice mail. Frantic, she got out of her car and jogged to the field, her heart in her throat. Where could they be? How could both of them not show up? Practice started in two minutes. They were always there ten minutes before it began.

She clenched her phone, ready to call Elliot's parents, then spotted the boy in right field. Rafe stood about twenty feet away.

Relieved, she slowed down. Then annoyance hit her full force. He had to have known she would notice his car wasn't there, since the three of them always waited for each other to walk down to the field together.

So much for optimism. Apparently all bets were off. Not only did he have no interest in working things out, he didn't even care about the friendship anymore.

Melina sank onto the bench in the dugout. It was the last place she wanted to be, especially when Beau moseyed over and leaned a shoulder against the dugout post. "So, Melina, I have it on good authority that you and Rafe aren't dating," he said casually.

That *good authority* probably being June, Melina thought. "We never said we were."

"Did you know there are bets being placed around town about you?"

She jumped up. "What?"

"Yep." He looked out over the field thoughtfully, then zeroed in on her, taking a long look at her standing there, flustered beyond speech. "A couple of 'em. One's for when you go out in public together for the first time. One's for when you get engaged."

She couldn't speak. They'd been so careful, too. Damn June Adams. She had to be the source of it all.

"Cat got your tongue, Melina?"

"It's too ridiculous to comment on."

"Uh-huh. That's why you sprang out of your seat

like a rocket, and your face is bright red." He cocked his head. "How's that saying go? The lady protests too much?"

She fumed silently, needing to protect her own image, but also protecting Elliot, whose future was in Beau's hands today. Today, of all days, wasn't the time to irritate him.

His grin was wide and leisurely. "By the way, I've invested in both pools, but I picked the same day for them to happen. Tomorrow. Don't let me down, okay?" He touched the brim of his cap and strode back out to where the team was gathered, waiting for him to fire his opening salvo about this being the last practice, the last chance to ask questions or improve a skill.

Melina made herself calm down enough to watch the practice, because it was the most important one of Elliot's young career. She found herself holding her breath as each grounder came toward him. He missed all of them.

Come on, Elliot, shine. Please shine, she urged him silently. Rafe seemed sure that he would make the team, but Melina thought Beau was a loose cannon, given to overreaction and delusions of grandeur. So she sat in the dugout, knees bouncing, fingers laced and numb from squeezing, her heart lodged in her throat.

Elliot got up to bat four times, connecting three times, and openly unhappy at himself for missing the fourth, drawing the gazes of the other kids by kicking the dirt and muttering to himself. However, Rafe called Elliot's name then gave him a run of hand signals, and he straightened his shoulders and went to stand next to his teammates waiting to bat, encouraging them by clapping, as the rest of the boys did.

Tears filled her eyes. How far he'd come. How very far. And it was all thanks to Rafe. She couldn't take any credit, nor could Beau as coach. Everything Elliot had learned about baseball, except for hitting, had come from Rafe.

Melina finally relaxed, her thoughts heading in a different direction. She wondered if Rafe knew about the bets.

She also wondered how many people had actually put money on them. She wished she found it funny, but mostly it was humiliating. Especially if she and Rafe didn't work things out—which looked more like a possibility now than it had before the practice started. Why hadn't he called and let her know he wouldn't be meeting her in the parking lot?

A total change in routine generally meant something.

As the practice wrapped up, Melina started winding up again, too. She was irritated at Rafe and annoyed at Beau—well, the whole town, actually, or at least those who'd placed bets on her and Rafe's hearts. Because that was what was happening—people were betting on whether or not she and Rafe would find love again—or break each other's hearts again.

Practice ended. She joined the team and coaches for their final pep talk. After, Beau pulled Rafe aside and said something privately to him. Rafe shook his hand, then started walking to the parking lot, inviting her along with his gaze.

"Elliot's all set for the big game tomorrow," Rafe said.

She wanted to whoop, jump and do the happy dance, but she couldn't, since Elliot hadn't known he might not be allowed to play. Nor could she hug him, because that kind of physical contact made him squirm.

"I'm looking forward to the game myself," she said. "Elliot, you've worked really hard. I'm so proud of you."

He grinned. They reached the parking lot.

"Where's your car?" she asked Rafe, trying to keep her cool.

"At home. I walked. Needed to blow off steam."

"And you didn't think to let me know of your change?" Okay, maybe she wasn't being so cool now.

He raised his brows. "It didn't occur to me. You found us."

"You always wait. Or I wait. We go together."

"I'm sor—"

"Did you know people have placed bets on us?" she asked, interrupting his apology, everything coming to a head for her.

He glanced at Elliot, who'd turned around and

gave them a worried look. "I did hear that, yes," Rafe said quietly.

"You *knew?* And you didn't bother to tell me? How could you not tell me? I found out from *Beau,* of all—"

"Stop it," Elliot said, putting his hands over his ears. "Stop yelling."

She hadn't been yelling. In fact, her voice was barely raised, but he, like many Asperger's kids, got sensory overload quickly, especially from sound. And especially when that sound was an argument, not a cheer.

He didn't wait for her apology but raced ahead to where his mother waited in the parking lot.

"What's wrong?" Debbie asked as Elliot stormed past her to climb right into the car and jerk the door shut. "Was there a problem? Did he not make—" She put a hand to her mouth.

"He's in," Rafe said immediately. "He made it. Melina and I were having a disagreement, and he got uncomfortable. I apologize."

"Me, too," Melina said. "It had nothing to do with Elliot, or even baseball. All my fault."

"Heavens, Melina." Debbie hugged her hard. "He hears us argue. It's another life lesson."

"Well, he needs to hear people apologize, too," Melina said, then opened the car door. He was already buckled in and staring out the windshield. "I'm sorry I raised my voice, Elliot. I'm sorry it made you uncomfortable."

He gave her a quick glance. "It's okay."

"Thank you. I'll see you tomorrow for the game. Would you mind if my family come? And probably Rafe's? Everyone would like to cheer your team on."

He thought about it for a few seconds. "That would be okay."

"Great. I'll see you then." She closed the door.

"Big day tomorrow," Debbie said.

"A very big day. He's ready," Rafe said.

Debbie hugged them both. "Thank you so much." She waved, hopped in the car and drove off.

"I'm sorry you were worried," Rafe said right away. "But, really, Melina, don't you think you overreacted?"

Of course she had. Her emotions were bubbling, her thinking not clear. Overreacting was par for the course under those circumstances. But she didn't like how paternal he'd just sounded, either.

Plus, she should've been on his mind. When it came down to it, *that* was what bothered her most.

"I can see where you might think that," she said, lifting her chin.

He smiled. "We're at an impasse about this. Can we just let it go?"

She didn't want to let it go. She should've been on his mind! But before she could find a point to argue, he said, "You've been at all the practices. What do you think? Is Elliot ready?"

"Skillwise, I know he still has a lot to learn, which

he will. But it's his self-control that's impressed me. What were the gestures you made when he was about ready to blow his top?"

"A reminder to calm down. I discovered he loves when the coaches give their run of hand signals when they're at bat. The more complicated, the better. He learned them faster and more consistently than the other boys, frankly. I added a couple just for him, but I bury them in decoy signals just for fun."

She clamped her mouth shut and contemplated him for a few long seconds. "Do you ever do anything wrong, Rafe?"

"What's that supposed to mean?"

"It's a simple question. You never seem to make a misstep. You say the right things. You sacrifice for a boy you don't know. You take care of your father."

He leaned close. "I make love pretty well, too."

She caught fire just from his words and the way he said them. "You're not exactly humble."

"See? Not perfect. My fatal flaw. Are you happy now?"

No. No, she wasn't happy. She'd thought she was getting there last night, but now she felt miserable. *You forgot about me,* she wanted to shout at him, but he'd already decided it was no big deal. Trying to convince him that it *was* a big deal would be useless. As far as he was concerned, they'd broken up. He wasn't obligated to do anything for her.

Disheartened at the thought, she said, "I should get going."

"Me, too." He was entirely too cheerful. "See you."

Off he went, leaving her with her teeth clenched and her irritation still brewing. So this was how it was going to be with them? He no longer sees when she's upset? And she gets upset easily?

This would require some thinking on her part.

She headed for her car then spotted Beau on his way to the office building. "Beau! Wait up."

She reached him quickly. "I just wanted to thank you for including Elliot on the team. It means a lot to all of us."

He lifted his cap and scratched his head. "Well, Melina, I don't think the boy's up to speed, but I can't fight city hall, you know? I've got a lot on the line here. I couldn't afford the press."

"What do you mean, you can't fight city hall? What press?"

"Rafe left you out of the loop? Well, isn't that interesting. Okay, then, I'm happy to tell you. He threatened me with a civil suit if I didn't leave the boy on the team. I can't afford a lawsuit, financially or professionally." He walked away, then turned back. "Rafe's got the kid under control, so you can sit in the stands during the game, if you want, instead of the dugout—or don't even show up, if you don't want to."

He left, his stride taking him a long distance in a brief time, as she stood watching him, thinking about what he'd said. When had Rafe threatened him? Yet another thing he hadn't discussed with her.

She got in her car and headed home, then spotted him walking down Main. She pulled over, lowered the window. "Want a ride?"

"I'm good, thanks." He kept walking so that she had to move slowly alongside him.

"I'd like to talk to you, Rafe."

"You're just going to chew me out. I'll pass."

She frowned. Today was the first time she'd been openly angry at him. She didn't think it was fair for him to act as if it was something she did all the time.

"I have things to tell you," she called out to him. "Need to tell you. Especially about my grandfather."

"I figured it out. It doesn't matter, Melina. Nothing from the past matters."

Blood drained from her head so that she was a little dizzy, because it did matter to her. The past and the present mattered.

And certainly the future.

When a car honked behind her, she picked up speed, but she didn't go home. Instead she drove to his home and pulled in the driveway. She was sitting on his front porch when he came up.

He eyed her, took out his keys and unlocked the door without saying anything, although he did leave the door open.

"I haven't seen your house yet," she said, following

him inside, but he was already out of sight. She followed sounds until she found him in the kitchen, his head in the refrigerator.

He tossed her a Coke, got a second one for himself. "Want some chips and salsa?" he asked.

"Sure." She sat at the counter, popped open her soda and took a sip. His kitchen was gorgeous, all stainless steel and granite, maple cabinets and beautiful tile.

"What do you think?" he asked, setting bowls on the counter, taking the seat beside her.

"Money well spent."

He clinked cans with her and took a long drink, then set down the can. "So."

"So?"

"You have things to say, I guess."

He seemed amused. And calm. And…tolerant. "Gramps admitted—"

"In the past. Choose another topic," he said.

She pursed her lips. "Beau told me you threatened him with a lawsuit."

"I did. Next question?"

Meaning, that was all he would say on the matter. Actually, Melina kind of admired him for that. He'd dealt with a situation that needed to be dealt with. Action did speak louder than words.

"Why didn't you tell me about the betting pool?" she asked.

"I figured it would tick you off."

"You decided I didn't need to know something that...infamous about myself?"

"I found out the day after we'd broken things off. I figured it wouldn't be relevant."

"After *you'd* broken things off," she said.

"I stand corrected."

She couldn't get a handle on him. He didn't seem happy she was there, but he also didn't seem angry. She finally just ran out of steam. He hadn't responded in a way that furthered their conversation. Now she was stuck sitting at his kitchen counter with nothing to say. She dipped a chip in some salsa and ate, the crunch sounding cannon-fire loud. So did he. They went through the bowl of chips without conversation. Then she was at a loss.

"I guess I should go," she said.

"Would you like to see the rest of the house?"

She still couldn't figure out his mood. He hadn't touched her, but hadn't given her the cold shoulder, either. "Yes, I would, thanks."

The tour didn't take long. He hadn't invested in dining room furniture yet, and had only a few pieces in the living room, wanting to wait until they'd finished repairing, staining and painting. His home office held only a desk and chair.

Upstairs, two bedrooms were empty and in sore need of fresh paint and window coverings. Another bedroom was furnished so that his father could stay overnight. Then came the master bedroom, which was remodeled and spectacular, the headboard tall and hand carved, the bedding colorful and inviting.

"I tore down the wall between this room and a bedroom beside it to make the master bath and walk-in closet," he said, letting her peek into both spaces. "Come see the view out the back window."

From there she could take in his entire backyard, a sprawling mess.

"I've lined up a crew to relandscape," he said. "They start next week. But picture this—a big deck with built-in barbecue right off the house. A swimming pool and spa over there. Lots of lawn."

"A place for a vegetable garden?" she asked. "And a dog or two?"

"It wouldn't be a home without them."

If Melina stayed in his bedroom for one more minute she would haul him off to his king-size bed and have her way with him.

He looked at his watch. "I've got a meeting I need to get ready for."

Just like that her decision was made. Or rather, taken away. She should be grateful, but...

"I'll see you at the game tomorrow," she said, even though the words hurt as they dragged along her throat. He'd been able to turn off the attraction switch way too easily.

They walked downstairs together. He opened the front door, held it as she passed by him. He didn't follow her to the car, but also didn't shut the door until she'd backed out and waved goodbye.

If his intention had been to let her know he was over her, he'd succeeded. He'd been nice—a horrible word, in this case. He'd invited her in, gave her food and drink, took her on a tour, then sent her on her way, all of it done in a nice, polite way.

She'd never been more discouraged in her life.

Sometimes what was broken couldn't be fixed— like this relationship. Giving up was foreign to her, but it looked as though she had to. He hadn't wanted to hear any details about Gramps. He'd already given up.

And there was no changing Rafe Mendoza's mind once it was made up.

Chapter Sixteen

The last day of March brought beautiful spring weather, the perfect start for the new baseball season. Seeing the stands filling up, Melina was torn between sitting in the dugout or on the benches with everyone else.

In the end, she was honest with herself, deciding that Elliot wouldn't care whether she was in the dugout or not. Plus the view was better from the stands.

People wandered into the complex, carrying hot dogs and popcorn, licorice and churros, the scents mingling in the air, adding to the excitement. Melina sat with Elliot's anxious parents. Soon her family arrived, then Rafe's father and brothers. Everyone who'd had a hand in helping Elliot had made time to come and support him.

His team, the Orioles, took the field to much applause and whoops, the boys acting cool, as if they didn't hear the cheering, and looking sharp in their brand-new uniforms and caps. Melina pressed a hand to her stomach.

"Me, too," her mother said, doing the same thing.

"Me, three," Elliot's mother said, laughing.

Melina already knew Elliot wouldn't play in the field until the fifth inning of the six-inning game, but every boy was in the batting lineup from the beginning to the end of the game. He would hit in the fourth spot, cleanup, which meant Beau counted on him to get base hits, to bring in the players on base ahead of him.

It was a lot of pressure. Elliot knew what hitting fourth meant.

The game started. Elliot stood at the chain-link fence of the dugout, watching, calling out support, with Rafe beside him, doing the same. There were hits and strikeouts, great throws and errors, shoe-string catches and dropped balls. The sun was in the eyes of the left and center fielders, causing missed catches, missed opportunities. Nerves showed. Coaches encouraged but also used errors as a time for instruction.

Elliot came up to bat, swung at the first pitch and missed. He looked for Rafe on the sidelines, got his it's-okay signal and stepped back into the batter's box. He hit the next ball over the shortstop's head, driving in the base runner at third to score, the stands exploding as people jumped up and hollered.

The game moved along, one team leading, then the other. Twice more Elliot came to the plate, getting two more singles, two more runs batted in. He went out to right field in the fifth inning but never had a ball hit to him.

Then came the bottom of the sixth and last inning. The Orioles were down by one run. There were two players on base. Elliot's batting average was .754, which meant he usually struck out or flied out once every four at bats. He was coming up on his fourth at bat. They needed him to connect now to at least tie the game.

The pressure intensified. Melina watched Elliot listen to Rafe, who was right in his face, before he headed to home plate. The crowd went quiet, too quiet.

Melina cupped her mouth with her hands and yelled, "You can do it, Elliot!"

Others followed suit—except his parents, who clutched each other and could barely watch.

"Strike one!" the umpire called.

Elliot backed away, looked at Rafe, got his signals.

Melina shouted, "Shake it off, Elliot. Shake it off."

He looked toward her for just a second. And in

that moment she knew that *she* mattered to him, too, not just Rafe. She plopped back down and pressed a hand to her mouth, overwhelmed. She was so glad he'd come into her life.

And because of him, she'd had Rafe for a while, too.

"What's wrong, honey?" her mother asked.

"Nothing, Mom. Everything's good. All good."

Another pitch. "Ball!"

Elliot stepped out but didn't look at Rafe, then he approached the plate again. "He calmed himself," Melina whispered excitedly to Elliot's mother. "He didn't rely on Rafe."

Debbie Anderson squeezed Melina's hand, knowing the importance of the moment. "We were blessed to find you and Rafe."

Melina grinned. "I don't know. You've been adopted by our families. You may regret that. We're big and we're noisy, you know."

"And Steve and I are grateful."

Elliot moved into the batter's box again. He set himself. His bat waggled a little then went still. The pitcher threw. Crack! The ball flew right at the second baseman, hit the tip of his outstretched glove and kept going into the field between center and right. One run scored, a second run scored. They won the game.

The stands erupted. Elliot's teammates mobbed him. Melina looked for signs of it being too much for him, but he was grinning and jumping up and down just like the rest of them.

Melina caught sight of Rafe watching the boys, a smile on his face, looking as proud as a father might. He lifted his gaze to hers, gave her a small salute, then dragged his cap down over his face for a minute, bringing tears to her eyes.

She wished she could wrap her arms around him and never let go.

Wouldn't that give everyone in town something to bet on? she thought, and finally laughed about it. Where else but in Small Town, America, could something like that happen.

And she was very glad she lived there.

Melina came to a decision—she was not going to give him up without a fight this time. If she was going to lose him, it wouldn't be because she hadn't made the effort. Time for one last hurrah before she called it quits.

Even if she had to do the proposing. At least then she would have answers.

Postgame pizza was a tradition after the first and last games of the season. After a little while, the noise proved to be too much for Elliot, whose parents decided to take him home before he was overwhelmed.

Rafe followed them to their car. "I'll see you at practice, okay, sport?"

Elliot nodded, then they did the seven-part handshake they'd made up. Steve and Debbie tried to thank him, but Rafe gave Elliot the credit and said he'd been privileged to give him some help along the way.

Rafe felt good. Worn out, but good. The game had sent him on a sentimental journey, especially hearing Melina yelling from the stands. It might as well have been him at the plate instead of Elliot, the memory was so vivid.

He headed back into the pizza parlor intending to tell people goodbye. He needed to make some phone calls, finalize some plans. The sooner, the better.

His cell phone rang—Ross Fortune.

"I figured you'd want to be kept in the loop," he said. "My brother Flint came to town this afternoon. He's had his DNA test already, so we should know soon if he's baby Anthony's father."

"Any word from Cooper?"

"No. He goes where the work is, and sometimes he doesn't get in touch for months. But the other big news is we just got a call from the Haggerty, Texas, police department. Seems they've got a homeless man with amnesia who may be William Fortune. Jeremy and Andrew are on their way now."

"So Jeremy was right to keep the faith about his father. That's great news." He saw Beau open the pizza parlor door and look out. Rafe waved him over. "Thanks for letting me know, Ross."

Rafe slipped the phone in his pocket and waited for Beau.

"You were right," Beau said seriously.

"So were you, Beau."

"About what?"

"He wasn't fully ready, except for hitting."

"But you're going to keep working with him, right?" Beau asked.

Rafe nodded. "You're a good coach, Beau. I've had my share of coaches, and you're one of the best."

Beau cleared his throat. "Thanks."

"And you were right about something else, too. I *was* jealous that you went to the show."

"You seem to have done okay," Beau said, smiling. "Besides, I heard you had offers after college."

Rafe didn't like to dwell on it. He'd stuck with his plan to go to law school, and most of the time could convince himself that he'd made the right choice. "A couple offers. I'm sorry about your injury." He didn't add any platitudes, knowing it wouldn't help.

"Me, too. But what are you gonna do, huh? Life goes on."

Rafe decided to change the subject. "I hear you started a betting pool on Melina and me."

Rafe's old rival grinned. "Some harmless entertainment. She looked a little peeved when she found out."

"You could say that."

"I noticed she's been short on feistiness lately, Rafe. Figured she could use a boost."

"Thanks."

Beau laughed at Rafe's dry tone, then he turned

serious. "I'm thinking about bringing on a partner. Interested?"

Rafe wondered how much it cost Beau to ask. "Not in a partnership, but I've got a good head for business, and I'd be happy to do some consulting work for you. You've got something unique in how you're running the complex. I think I could help you grow it, maybe even franchise it. First thing you'd have to do is give up micromanaging. It'll take a lot of pressure off you."

Beau stuck out his hand, but seemed incapable of speech. Rafe shook it, then watched him return to the restaurant and his noisy, victorious team. Before the door shut all the way, Melina slipped out.

"I wondered where you went," she said, approaching him. Like many of the parents, she'd bought an Orioles T-shirt. The yellow color suited her. "Is Elliot okay?"

"He's pretty wiped out, I think." He'd wanted to get away without talking to her. He had places to go and people to meet, and he was afraid he'd get swept up into something with her before he was ready to. "I am, too. I'm going to go."

Her brows went up. "You can't even talk to me for a minute? I'm that repulsive to you now?"

"Repulsive? What the hell are you talking about?"

"You couldn't wait to get me out of your house yesterday. You didn't say one word to me after the game. And now you were going to leave without even saying goodbye or discussing Elliot for a minute—our common cause who will continue to be one until baseball season ends?" She crossed her arms. "What else am I supposed to think? You can't stand to be around me."

"You're wrong about that, but I don't have the time or energy to debate it with you right now. I have things to do, Melina. Important things." And the clock was ticking.

Hurt settled in her eyes. "I see. Well, at least you admit I'm unimportant."

He couldn't stand it. "You're important," he said. "Too important."

"How can someone be too important? I don't even know what that means. I don't see how the way you've been acting the past few days shows that I'm important in any way."

Melina was goading him on purpose. She'd been sitting in the pizza parlor watching people look from her to Rafe and back again constantly. Everyone wanted to know where things stood with them, but even she didn't know. And she was tired of being left in the dark herself. She was losing sleep and losing weight. She wanted to know where she stood and be able to move on.

If she proposed to him, she would know, one way or another. Except she hadn't planned on starting an argument, hadn't planned on him not wanting to spend even a second with her.

He glared at her. "You don't think you're important, Melina Lawrence? I'll show you how wrong you are."

He grabbed her hand and pulled her along, heading toward his car, unlocking it and waiting impatiently while she got inside. People were gathering outside the restaurant door, a hum of excitement running through the ever-enlarging crowd.

"You're ruining everything, you know," he said, grinding out the words. "What happened to the patience you're so famous for? Two days. You only needed to wait two days." He slammed her door shut, ran around to the driver's side and got in.

Melina decided not to say anything. It seemed she'd unintentionally interrupted a plan he'd made, and she was now going to pay for it. Once again, had she hurt her own cause?

Usually when he got mad, he got quiet. He would speak without emotion, always being logical. Now he was acting so irrationally she didn't know what to make of it. Except that she recognized she'd chosen the wrong moment to force him into some kind of action where she was concerned. Apparently he'd had a strategy in mind....

He drove a few blocks, turned onto Main, pulled up alongside a rundown wooden-sided building. The old Crockett building. *Their* building.

"Recognize this place?" he asked.

"Of course I do."

He stared at it. "This used to be our future."

"At Angie's wedding reception you said you thought it should've been torn down by now."

He frowned. "No, I didn't. I said I was surprised it hadn't been." He angled toward her. "I bought it. Or more accurately, I'm in the process of buying it."

"Why?"

"Because I'm opening an office in Red Rock. Right here."

He got out of the car, so she did, too. He shook his head at her, probably because she hadn't waited for him to open the door, then he led her to a window and peered inside.

"If you'd been patient for a couple more days," he said, annoyance in his voice, "I would've had it cleaned up, and a nice table set, and an elegant meal brought in. After dinner, I would've pulled out a black-velvet box, gotten down on one knee and asked you to marry me."

She barely reacted to his words, not fully comprehending them, her own goal crowding out his. Her plans had gone awry, too. "Yeah? Well, I was going to propose to you, then I got scared, so I got mad."

They faced each other like duelists.

"Wait. What?" she asked. "You were going to propose?"

"The right way. The romantic way." He shoved his hands through his hair. "I can't believe I just let that happen. I should've walked away at the pizza parlor. Done things the way I wanted to, was planning to."

She crossed her hands over her chest, which ached.

"I love you, Rafe." She took a step toward him, happiness pouring into her, out of her. "I love you with all my heart."

He took her by the shoulders. "I love you more, Melina. Once I let go of the anger, love filled the empty space so fast I could barely breathe. I thought you only wanted sex, and I wanted that, too, but I also only wanted *you*. Anyway I could get you." He looked amused and surprised at the same time. "*You* were going to propose?"

She laughed joyously. "I'd already waited years for you. I didn't want to wait a second longer. And I wanted a definite answer, not more could'ves and should'ves."

He kissed her then, softly, tenderly but thoroughly. "So, marry me today."

"Today? Rafe, really—"

"We've lost too much time already. We'll fly to Vegas."

Melina threw her arms around him, laughing and crying, happier than she'd been in such a long time. "Not today, but very soon. I want a real wedding, with our families and friends. Not a big one, but a proper one. I've dreamed of it since I was fourteen."

He threaded his fingers through her hair. "I'll give you a month. Let's go tell our families."

"That's a deal. I can— Oh, no! No, we can't get engaged today." She looked around, wondering if anyone had seen them—then could barely count the number of cars that had pulled up. "The bet, Rafe. The bet."

He eyed the street and the people standing outside their cars, watching. "I love this woman!" he shouted. "I just asked her to marry me and she said yes!" Then he bent her over his arm and kissed her most publicly, most exhaustively.

"Pay up, people!" came Beau's voice out of the melee.

Car horns honked. Cheers went up.

"Bells are ringing," Rafe said, holding her tight. "For me and my girl."

"Our song." She framed his face with her hands, cherishing him, sorry that she'd taken away his big proposal moment. She would make it up to him. "Let's go tell our families before the grapevine beats us to it."

"I love you," he said, taking her hand to walk her to his car, to start their lives together.

"I love you more," she said, echoing him from earlier.

It was a good start.

* * * * *

Look for FORTUNE'S JUST DESSERTS,
the next book in
THE FORTUNES OF TEXAS:
LOST...AND FOUND
Coming next month to Silhouette Special Edition.

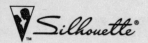
Silhouette®

COMING NEXT MONTH

Available March 29, 2011

SPECIAL EDITION

REQUEST YOUR FREE BOOKS!

2 FREE NOVELS PLUS 2 FREE GIFTS!

SPECIAL EDITION
Life, Love and Family!

YES! Please send me 2 FREE Silhouette Special Edition® novels and my 2 FREE gifts (gifts are worth about $10). After receiving them, if I don't wish to receive any more books, I can return the shipping statement marked "cancel." If I don't cancel, I will receive 6 brand-new novels every month and be billed just $4.24 per book in the U.S. or $4.99 per book in Canada. That's a saving of at least 15% off the cover price! It's quite a bargain! Shipping and handling is just 50¢ per book in the U.S. and 75¢ per book in Canada.* I understand that accepting the 2 free books and gifts places me under no obligation to buy anything. I can always return a shipment and cancel at any time. Even if I never buy another book, the two free books and gifts are mine to keep forever.

235/335 SDN FC7H

Name	(PLEASE PRINT)
Address	Apt. #
City	State/Prov. Zip/Postal Code

Signature (if under 18, a parent or guardian must sign)

Mail to the **Reader Service:**
IN U.S.A.: P.O. Box 1867, Buffalo, NY 14240-1867
IN CANADA: P.O. Box 609, Fort Erie, Ontario L2A 5X3

Not valid for current subscribers to Silhouette Special Edition books.

Want to try two free books from another line?
Call 1-800-873-8635 or visit www.ReaderService.com.

* Terms and prices subject to change without notice. Prices do not include applicable taxes. Sales tax applicable in N.Y. Canadian residents will be charged applicable taxes. Offer not valid in Quebec. This offer is limited to one order per household. All orders subject to credit approval. Credit or debit balances in a customer's account(s) may be offset by any other outstanding balance owed by or to the customer. Please allow 4 to 6 weeks for delivery. Offer available while quantities last.

Your Privacy—The Reader Service is committed to protecting your privacy. Our Privacy Policy is available online at www.ReaderService.com or upon request from the Reader Service.

We make a portion of our mailing list available to reputable third parties that offer products we believe may interest you. If you prefer that we not exchange your name with third parties, or if you wish to clarify or modify your communication preferences, please visit us at www.ReaderService.com/consumerschoice or write to us at Reader Service Preference Service, P.O. Box 9062, Buffalo, NY 14269. Include your complete name and address.

SSE11

Selene wanted nothing to do with the father of her son, Alex; but Aristedes had other plans...that included them.

Read on for an sneak peek from
THE SARANTOS SECRET BABY by Olivia Gates,
available April 2011, only from Harlequin Desire.

"You were right to turn my marriage offer down," Aristedes said.

And Selene found her voice at last, found the words that would not betray the blow he'd dealt her. "Thanks for letting me know. You didn't have to come all the way here, though. You could have just let it go. I left yesterday with the understanding that this case is closed."

Before the hot needles behind her eyes could dissolve into an unforgivable display of stupidity and weakness, she began to close the door.

The door stopped against an immovable object. His flat palm.

"I can't accept that." His voice was low, leashed.

What did her tormentor mean now? Was he ending one game only to start another?

She raised eyes as bruised as her self-respect to his, found nothing there but solemnity and determination.

Before she could voice her confusion, he elaborated. "I never let anything go unless I'm certain it's unworkable. I realize I made you an unworkable offer, and that's why I'm withdrawing it. I'm here to offer something else. A workability study."

She leaned against the door, thankful for its support and partial shield. "Your son and I are not a business venture you can test for feasibility."

His gaze grew deeper, made her feel as if he was trying to delve into her mind, take control of it. "It's actually the other way around. I'm the one who would be tested."

She shook her head. "Why bother? I know—and *you* know—you're not workable. Not with me."

His spectacular eyebrows lowered over eyes she felt were emitting silver hypnosis. "You're right again. Neither you nor I have any reason to believe that isn't the truth. The only truth. It might be best for both you and Alex to never hear from me again, to forget I exist. But then again, maybe not. I'm only asking for the chance for both of us to find out for certain. You believe I'm unworkable in any personal relationship. I've lived my life based on that belief about myself. I never really had reason to question it. But I have one now. In fact, I have two."

Find out what happens in
THE SARANTOS SECRET BABY by Olivia Gates,
available April 2011, only from Harlequin Desire.

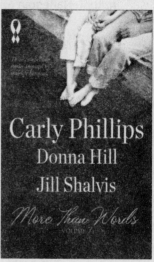